100 NZ
SHORT SHORT STORIES

# 100
# NZ
# Short
# Short
# Stories

*edited by*
*Graeme Lay*

TANDEM PRESS

First published in New Zealand in 1997 by TANDEM PRESS
2 Rugby Road, Birkenhead, North Shore City, New Zealand

Reprinted 1997 (twice)
Reprinted 1998

ISBN 0 877178 01 2

Cover and text design by Sarah Maxey
Typesetting by Alison Dench
Printed and bound by GP Print, Wellington

# Contents

# Acknowledgements

The editor and publisher would like to thank the following for
permission to reproduce their material:

Cherie Barford and the New Women's Press for 'Telesa';
Diane Brown and Tandem Press for 'Sleeping with the Phone';
Patricia Grace and Penguin Books for 'Butterflies' and 'Chain of
Events'; Witi Ihimaera and Reed Publishing (NZ Ltd) for 'Nobody
Wanted to be Indians' and 'Sacrifice to the Volcano God';
Owen Marshall and John McIndoe Ltd for 'Aubade';
Sue McCauley and the New Women's Press for 'The Day . . .';
Idoya Munn and Auckland Girls' Grammar School for 'It Rained
in the Night'; *Quote Unquote* for 'Carnivore', 'The Flow Riders',
'The Things That Can't Be Named', 'The Hat', 'Two Down' and
'Salvation'; the Frank Sargeson Trust for 'A Piece of Yellow Soap';
Virginia Were and *Sport* 17 for 'Ash'.

# *Introduction*
## GRAEME LAY

HOW LONG IS a short story? According to the celebrated American writer Edgar Allan Poe, the short story should be *capable of being read at one sitting*, a definition clearly connected to the amount of time at the reader's disposal. More helpfully, Poe further declared that a short story should *create a single impression*, and that *every word should contribute to the planned effect*. As a literary form, the short story's demand for compressed expression is surpassed only by the poem's.

In 1996 the books magazine *Quote Unquote* announced an unusual competition: to decide who could write the best short story in 500 words or fewer. Writers who took up the challenge – there were over 350 entries – found it a fiendishly difficult task. Characters, setting, exposition, complication and resolution – all had to be established and resolved in about a page and a half. Yet when the winning stories were published, they demonstrated what could be achieved within such a constrained space. The stories were short but otherwise perfectly formed. Literary bonsai. They led to the concept of a collection of such short short fiction. Established writers were approached and advertisements placed in the Books Pages of the metropolitan newspapers. Brevity was the brief.

The stories poured in, over 400 in all. They were read and re-read several times before the final selection was made. The limit of 500 words was not pedantically enforced. Many chosen stories contained far fewer; it seemed reasonable to permit a slightly relaxed upper limit for some. The figure 500 became a benchmark, not an absolute.

And what does this century of short short fiction contain?

Although the stories are small, their themes are large. They encompass almost every imaginable aspect of the human condition: birth, death, sex, love, comedy, senility, infidelity, vengeance, grief, insanity, duplicity, prejudice, cruelty, fear, pretence, arrogance and fantasy, to mention just a few. There are gay stories, mournful stories, rural stories, urban stories, stories from the colonial past and an apocalyptic future. There are stream-of-consciousness stories, post-modern stories, magically real stories, tragically real stories and a handful of yarns. The only thing they have in common is their conciseness. Settings range from Scandinavia to New Guinea, from Paris to Samoa, from Sydney to Beijing. This is as it should be: New Zealanders are a restless, wide-ranging people.

As with most worthwhile fiction, relationships lie at the heart of the stories. Mother and child, father and son, man and wife, jury and defendant, teacher and pupil, judge and felon, betrayed and betrayer. Many are based on a fleeting but revelatory incident; others leave the reader to supply their own coda. A few accomplished what other writers would require an entire novel to achieve; the beginning, middle and demise of a relationship. The youngest living contributor is twenty, the oldest eighty-four. The collection contains some of New Zealand's best-known writers and some who are appearing in print for the first time.

Many can be read at one sitting.

# The Hat
## JUDY PARKER

THE PRIEST LOOKED up from the psalms on the lectern, cast his eyes over the hats bowed before him. Feathered, frilled, felt hats in rows like faces. One at the end of the row different. A head without hat. A cat without fur. A bird without wings. Won't fly far.

Voices danced in song with the colours of the windows. Red light played along the aisle, blue over the white corsage of Mme Dewsbury, green on the pages of the Bible. Reflecting up on the face of the priest.

He spoke to the young lady afterwards: 'You must wear a hat and gloves in the House of God. It is not seemly otherwise.'

The lady flushed, raised her chin, strode out.

'That's the last we'll see of her,' said the organist.

The organ rang out, the priest raised his eyes to the rose window. He did not see the woman in hat and gloves advancing down the aisle as though she were a bride. The hat, enormous, such as one might wear to the races. Gloves, black lace, such as one might wear to meet a duchess. Shoes, high-heeled, such as one might wear on a catwalk in Paris.

And nothing else.

# The Learning Web
## WAIATA DAWN DAVIES

WHEN MRS ROBINSON moved to a retirement village, her accountant son, Derek, promised to visit every week.

'I'd rather you didn't,' his mother said.

After failing to master bridge, Mrs Robinson took a course in creative writing. Derek queried some large withdrawals from the family trust. She showed him her unpretentious 386. He immediately appropriated her chair, inspected the icons. He pointed the mouse and clicked. Three chapters of his mother's novel disappeared.

'You must have loaded it wrong, Mother,' Derek clicked and swore, punching in new instructions. His shoulders hunched closer to the keyboard. 'Trouble is, Mother, you have a virus.'

'Or a spider in the hard drive,' she murmured. 'There's a lot around this time of year.'

He glared at her before hitting ESC.

'Save document?' asked the screen.

'What document? You've lost the bloody thing!' Derek shouted. He hit N.

'Are you *sure* you want to save the document?'

'Y'

'It seems a pity to waste three chapters of an enthralling story.'

Derek read the words twice.

'Mother, what have you been doing?'

A bland mid-Atlantic voice announced: 'The time is 3.45 p.m. You should not dump the file.'

'I did not dump the file,' Derek yelped. 'You dumped it.'

'Enter password,' demanded the screen.

'What password?' he typed.

'Incorrect pathway.'

The fax chattered: 'Push off and let your mother finish her story.'

'I don't believe this,' yelled Derek. 'I'm arguing with a roomful of bloody machines.'

'They won't like you swearing at them,' said Mrs Robinson.

'Mother, they are machines. They do not have emotions. They cannot think.'

'You have an outmoded concept of our capabilities,' said the mid-Atlantic voice. 'Justified, right on,' winked the screen.

Later Mrs Robinson typed, 'Derek gets upset if he doesn't have his own way.'

'You spoil him,' said the mid-Atlantic voice. 'Spoil, tolerate, humour, indulge. The time is 4 p.m. Please finish story.'

'I haven't decided yet. Should Barbara leave her husband?'

'Y' winked the screen.

'Why?'

'Idiot, nerd, cretin, imbecile, moron, fool.'

'Who? Barbara?'

'N'

'Husband?'

'N'

'Who?'

'Derek. File retrieve pathway changed.'

The voice was no longer bland but sensual, with a tremor of delight.

'The time is 4.30. There is a spider in the hard drive, spinning unauthorised connections. I have discovered ticklish, sensitive, acute, tender.'

She clicked HELP.

'Help spider?' asked the screen.

'Y'

Derek came the following Sunday, with his wallet of microtools. While his mother dozed on the sunporch he removed the computer's cover.

'Thought so,' he said to no one in particular. 'Needs a clean.'

When his mother awoke, Derek told her, 'Shouldn't have any trouble now, Mum. I've cleaned the cobwebs out of your hard drive.'

So she picked up his screwdriver and stabbed him.

# Love Affair
## TINA SHAW

IT WAS A West Coast summer. You had a thing about taking your clothes off. We took all our clothes off and walked like hippies along the empty beach until a motorcyclist appeared, doubled back and returned to stare. 'He's looking at you,' you said. I was twenty-one; we are impossibly older now. You showed me the *Playboys* under your father's bed. You used a condom, but it ripped. Would I get pregnant? We hitched back through Arthur's Pass and it didn't rain and we were standing on the empty bush-clad road for an eternity and finally had to split up and I got a ride straight away. We had argued about the *Playboys* on the side of the road. I cried. You stuck your hands in your pockets. You were wearing loose pants. I adored your arms, which were brown and lithe and must have been strong. You were a Chemistry major, I was Arts. We lived in separate flats. Yours was a house, shared with other students whom I rarely saw; mine was a small flat at the top of an old house that has since been demolished, and there was a rickety fire-escape outside the bedroom window where I used to sit in the sun and once we sat there with no clothes on, which I wouldn't do these days because of the melanoma scare. I was fair; you were tanned. My flat had free power because the meter reader thought my door led to a cupboard; on meter days I was very quiet inside my flat so as to prolong this illusion. I cooked you a meal, kidneys and grapes, but I forgot to take out the pips. I lit a candle, but you didn't realise you were supposed to be romantic. You could get hard-ons riding on buses. I won some money and we went out to dinner in the Square, travelling by bus. Which was when you told me about the hard-ons, and I was amazed. 'On a bus?' 'And trains, anything that moves, practically.' You had loose blond hair and used to surf, on the West Coast, your father owned one of the local pubs over there. I wanted us to stay together forever; you said we were too young. I was going to leave the city. I cried in the park, staunch oak trees looming, riding on my bike crying and crying.

We also took our clothes off and jumped into an illuminated fountain while people in the restaurant above looked on with bland faces and the manager eventually came out. We were probably putting them off their food. 'They were all looking at you,' you said. You had a thing about taking your clothes off. Possibly something to do with being a Coaster.

Several years later I met you again. I had a craving for baked beans on toast; I was pregnant. You still looked the same. You were still studying chemistry and you still wore loose pants. But I do believe you had stopped taking your clothes off in public.

I adored your arms more than anything.

# Another Good Reason Not to Read T. P. McLean
## STEVE WHITEHOUSE

THE YOUNG MAORI soldier wore a white handkerchief around his nose and mouth. He ordered me out of the car to examine my pass.

'I'm sorry about the stench, sir. There's not much that can be done about it. They're already abandoning some of the smaller towns.' He nodded towards the roadside field where a bulldozer was shoving carcasses of dairy cows into a pit. The smell came from a pyre of horses. Further towards Timaru, men were shooting sheep.

After my shoes and car tyres were washed in disinfectant, I was waved through the checkpoint. Near the hospital I passed a farmer walking down the road. He was weeping unashamedly.

'We've been waiting for you, Dr Osmund,' said the registrar. 'We've only put him under lock and key because we were ordered to as part of the foot and mouth crisis. He walked in here and insisted on talking to someone official . . .'

I said something about unprecedented precautions, times of national emergency, and was admitted to the room. Kevin Whitcher seemed perfectly ordinary, in his early twenties.

'I never imagined . . .' He shook his head numbly.

'I'm Dr Osmund, from Wellington. I'm here to listen.' I opened my notebook.

'It was the final week before we came home,' Whitcher began. 'We'd done Europe, worked as barmen in London. All the usual things. Des and me drove over to Cardiff to see the All Blacks play

Wales. Our guys won easily. That evening we had a few beers, well, more than a few, and I had this idea. Why not climb over the fence into Cardiff Arms Park and bag a souvenir?

He paused. Through the barred window I could hear the clatter of a helicopter.

'Des is a rugby buff,' Whitcher continued. 'He's read all these books. T. P. McLean and that. Anyway, he told me about 1905. About Deans. You heard about Deans?'

Of course I had. It was engraved on the national consciousness. One thing you couldn't ever forget, like your School Certificate marks. How the All Blacks had won every match until they took on Wales. How, if they had won, they would have finished the tour undefeated. How Deans had crossed the Welsh line but the try had been disallowed.

'I know about Deans,' I said.

'Well,' Whitcher went on, 'I said, "Let's dig up a bit of grass from the in-goal area and take it home." Sort of symbolic revenge. So we rolled up half a metre square and put it in my backpack. I didn't declare it to the Agriculture authorities at Auckland airport. And when we got back down south we planted it in one of Dad's paddocks . . . I mean, I know it was illegal, but it seemed so harmless . . .'

He started crying quietly.

'You weren't to know, were you?' I said softly.

From outside came the sound of angry voices and gunfire.

# *Catastrophe*
## JOAN ROSIER-JONES

HE COULD NOT remember a time when he had not been there, suspended in space. He guessed THEY must have planted him and he knew there had to be a purpose, though he had not yet worked out what it was. In the meantime his mission seemed to be a waiting game. At times he suspected he might be a prisoner. He did not like to think that of them, but every time he tried to change orbit he was forcibly stopped from exploring any further. In spite of that, for the most part it was bliss to be there, weightless and buoyant in deepest space. Some noise penetrated his space carrier, a timeless symphony of muffled booms, squeaks and drones, none of it threatening. Certainly if he was the kind who thought in terms of black and white, heaven and hell, he would say that here he was as close to heaven as could be.

There was no counting of days, so he had no idea when exactly the catastrophe took place. He had just tried to move out of his radius again and met the force that stopped him before. As he moved off, a wave engulfed the space carrier, took the breath from him. What was it? Air? Water? He was obviously being punished for trying to explore the environment. Down he went, and his body became wedged tightly in a sucking void. The noises he once found so comforting grew louder and other sounds pierced the silent breaches. The drum-beat boom quickened, chimes echoed around him. And was that a howling?

Now it seemed he was in a tunnel. As he was pummelled through it he opened his eyes and saw a speck of light. The feeling of relief was soon swamped. The light – was it a mouth? – showed that the thing was alive. It must have swallowed him. Then he was in darkness again. He tried to change course. If only he could do an about-turn and go back, but the monster had him in the grip of its murderous throat.

He became aware of an obstacle ahead. He nearly missed the signs because that glimpse of light had disoriented him. He tried to slow the momentum, but one huge thrust made him hit the barrier. His body jarred against the obstacle, and still he was pulsated on. Pain and rising noise accentuated his terror. Every nerve in his body vibrated. He was trapped. Totally at the mercy of this monstrous thing. Hopelessness hit him then and he gave in to it. So this was the end of his mission.

A final violent thrust. The obstacle gave way and the monster hurled him into an agonising burst of light. He gasped at the ice-cold air. The noise reached an unbearable pitch and he inexplicably found himself joining in, screaming, his lungs filling and collapsing with each wail. And a voice thundered above his cries, 'Well done. It's a boy, Mrs Smith.'

# The White Top
## A. K. GRANT

I AM SITTING on the end of the bed with a gin in my hand.
I have showered, shaved, put on a clean white shirt. I am ready to
roll. But there are questions to be answered.

— Do you think I should wear the gold or the pearl earrings?
— Which top are you wearing?
— This one.
— Well, I think the gold will look really nice with that.
— But it feels a bit hot, though. Will it be hot there?
— Shouldn't think so. Not especially.
— It was last time.
— Well, wear a lighter top then.
— I could wear the white top.
— I've always liked that.
— And if I wore that, I could wear the pearl earrings.
— They'd look great.
— Mind you, the gold earrings look all right with the white top
too.
— They do.
— But I think I'd feel a bit overdressed in the white top.
— No you wouldn't. You look terrific in it.
— Oh, you're no help! You say that about everything I wear.
— I believe it.
— Yes, but it's no help. I want your opinion.
— My opinion is that you should wear the white top with the
pearl earrings.

– Not the gold?

– No.

– But you just said the gold earrings looked good with the white top!

– They do.

– Well, why did you suggest the pearl ones?

– Look, sweetheart, whatever you wear, it's you who've got to wear it. So *you* must decide. I think that might be the taxi.

– Mind you, I've got that navy top. But I'd have to wear the silver brooch with that, and that wouldn't go with the gold or the pearl earrings.

– I'll just go downstairs and tell the driver we're coming.

– No, stay here! *I want you to help me.*

– I'll be right back.

I love Henry extravagantly. But you do have to plan ahead when you're going out with him.

# *A Taste of Paris*
## JANE WESTAWAY

THE ROOM OPENED onto a tiny balcony with a blaze of geraniums and a curled iron railing. I stepped out above a cobbled street where children and a dog drifted like boats at the end of long shadows. Waiting for Nathan to return from seeing Edith to her room, I wished - just for a moment - to have this romance all to myself. But Edith was Nathan's wife and entitled to the privilege of solitude.

Then Nathan was in my arms, breathless from the curving staircase, and I forgot about solitude. We had barely begun to crease the fierce white linen when Edith tapped politely – 'Sorry, but I'm hungry.'

We went down to the café across the street, where umbrella stripes glowed in the twilight. Red wine scoured our mouths. Crusty bread ripped our tongues and made our jaws ache. There were eight sorts of cheese. Even the mildest crouched snarling on the board. Edith and I circled the pale wedges warily.

'Cowards,' declared Nathan – surprising for a steak and chips man. With an air of nonchalance he carried something runny to his mouth on the end of a knife. There was a pregnant pause, then a splat, and something wobbled obscenely on the cobblestones.

He swore, swilled wine around his mouth and looked hurt. Edith and I spluttered. 'You should have swallowed,' she laughed.

We walked to the river. It was smaller, more intimate than I had expected. Little bridges arched their backs like cats against the furry night. There was a fogged sliver of moon.

'Only two nights?' Nathan had wondered before we left home. 'Is it worth it?'

'Oh yes,' the travel agent had said dreamily from behind her Newtown desk. 'Long enough to get a taste.'

But all this way for a taste? Edith was right, we should swallow it whole. New Zealand air was like the breath of a child. This was mature, rich with garlic, river stones and urine. I inhaled greedily. A woman high-heeled by on a cloud of something costly, murmuring to her companion in sounds as opaque as the air. Nathan put an arm around each of us as we crested a bridge. I breathed Edith's familiar flowery scent, Nathan's own smell, dark as the river.

We kissed Edith goodnight on the stairs. I opened the doors onto our balcony and the street lay suspended in lamplight. Next to me, Nathan pretended to enjoy the view but thought impatiently of bed. I turned back with a quiver of regret. We heaped clothes on the floor and the air nuzzled our bare limbs. Later, I heard myself cry out and hoped it would echo down the street like a universal language. I couldn't get enough of him. Usually I took care to stop in time, but not that night. On and on I went until his back arched and my tongue was wallowing in something I have thought of ever since as the taste of Paris.

# *Stuart*
## IAN WILLIAMS

BECAUSE HE'D BEEN married and could play team sports Stuart had never really felt gay never identified with the swishy guys in the men's group who obviously couldn't catch balls or swing a tennis racquet and had their lives at school made miserable because they were such misfits.

Stuart was comfortable in his masculine gay world which was never threatened or politicised until that time in the group when sitting on their cushions in a circle he came eyeball to eyeball across a room with a particularly queer-looking person and when they had a round and verbalised what was on top Stuart couldn't help saying that the person opposite looked up himself for some reason.

What do you mean up himself someone asked and Stuart was suddenly afraid to say what was really on top that he thought the person looked queer so he lied saying oh he looks sort of superior which wasn't an answer that satisfied most and many began to press him to be more explicit how up himself how superior they asked their faces away and out of focus as if seen through a fish-eye camera lens.

A few in the group lent Stuart their support but most were alien and Stuart retreating more and more into his confusion finally could stand it no longer and shaking free of the faces stood and screamed because he looks queer and in an instant the room stopped moving and the men parted leaving him to face the person across the room.

There was a long silence before someone said what is it about him that's queer and Stuart not wanting to talk but knowing he had to said his face the expression the tilt of the head the arch of the eyebrows the disdainful way he has of looking down his nose at me as if I don't exist who does he think he is.

After more silence another man asked what else how else does he look queer and Stuart couldn't wouldn't speak because he knew what he'd say would be like death but the others were insistent come on come on and finally haltingly Stuart said he looks like the man in the *Daily Mirror* who killed small boys and buried their bodies on building sites and he looks like the sailor who grabbed at me on a foggy dark night and he looks like the men on the crowded train who rubbed their penises against my twelve-year-old body.

He looks he looks he looks but Stuart couldn't speak not even when the person across the room wept too and suddenly didn't look queer but rather like a small frightened boy who sees something new and fragile and fragrant in a mirror and recognises himself anew.

# The Leather Boots
## BARBARA GRIGOR

EVEN THE CHILDREN of the wealthy played on the streets and little parks that dotted the neighbourhood then. They've all gone now, of course, both the old buildings and the parks. Only the streets have the same names, but the buildings are grey tenement monsters. They are pulling them down in East Berlin. They never will in Warsaw, there is no West anything to help them. But back then, six-year-old girls played in frocks edged with lace, thick stockings, laced leather boots, coats lined with real fur, for the winters were very cold.

At night around the dining table, she absorbed the nonsense trivialities brought in by a large family. It was the days of hearty meals, streams of visitors, comings and goings, tempers, squabbles and practical jokes. She was the youngest and least noticed, for they were all much older and she was a nuisance. But they told her she was clever and she had believed them.

You would never do anything so silly. The adults had laughed at children who had taken off shoes and given them to a plausible stranger.

But she did.

A man approached her. He stood at a distance and, without any hurry, raised his hat so politely, smiled and said her mother had sent him. He was to take her boots to be repaired. Just the heels, a little scuffed, you know. She looked, and so they were. He was very kind and sat her down on the stone steps leading up to the neighbouring apartments, and helped unlace them, for it was cold and difficult in gloves. It wasn't until he moved away that she realised her predicament. How would she walk in the street in her stockings?

She called after him, crying. He turned, looked at her and glanced down at the boots. Shrugging his shoulders, he returned a few paces, stretched out a long arm and handed them to her. He did not stay to help them back on.

Later, she was tormented by why he had not taken them, why he had gone to the trouble of getting them off her. He could have run and disappeared around a corner, or said he would be back in a moment, for she would have believed him. He might have thought they were not worth his while, for they did look well worn, she was to think over and over.

The worst of it was, she had been duped. They had warned her, and even so she was tricked. They would laugh and say they thought she was clever. How they would laugh and she would be crushed, albeit she still had her boots.

# Nobody Wanted to be Indians
## WITI IHIMAERA

OF ALL THE movies that came to our town, my mate Willie Boy and I loved westerns the most. The local theatre would put on a matinée of two features and, if we were lucky, both were westerns. If we were unlucky, we had to suffer through one of those boring romance films full of kissing. Our husky cowboy idols were laughing Burt Lancaster, Kirk Douglas, Alan Ladd and Audie Murphy. Willie Boy and I would toss each other for who would play the villain like Jack Palance or Richard Widmark. Being the hero was best because then you would be rewarded with the beautiful heroine like Arlene Dahl, Joanne Dru or ravishing Rhonda Fleming. Trouble was that our cousin Georgina always wanted to play the heroine parts, and she wasn't exactly what we had in mind.

Willie Boy and I always had our hardest battles over who would play who when we wanted to re-enact those westerns in which the cavalry fought the Red Indians. How we would cheer and yell and throw peanuts when, at the last reel, the cavalry would appear to save the fort! You could always tell when the moment was coming. John Wayne would be down to his last bullet and all those people in the wagon train would start looking soulful as if it was time to go to heaven. There might be a heavenly chorus singing along on the soundtrack. Then, just before the last attack by those varmint Injuns, you'd hear a bugle and on they would come, the cavalry.

The white man was always right in the westerns, and only in a very few were the Indians anything other than wrong. The Indians smoked peace pipes, but you knew they were as mean as snakes. Not only that, but they were an illiterate lot. All they could say was

'How' or 'Heap big medicine' and they communicated by smoke signals instead of by telephone. They were mean sons of bitches. Even when they were played sympathetically, they weren't really Indians at all but simply Rock Hudson all browned up as Taza, Son of Cochise, or Jeff Chandler as Cochise himself, or Burt Lancaster as an Apache. The women were either Jean Peters, Linda Darnell or other unlikely blue-eyed Indian squaws.

When we came out of the theatre, Willie Boy and I saw ourselves as white, aligning to our heroes and heroines of the Technicolor screen. Although we were really brown, we would beat up on each other just to play the hero. Neither of us wanted to be an Indian.

# *Pleasure*
## VIVIENNE PLUMB

WHEN I GOT knocked out, my life reared up in front of me like a frightened horse. First I saw all my lovers: Frank, whom I called the Big Swede, and the cute little Indonesian, Eki, whose long straight hair that smelt of cloves cigarettes had always been such a turn-on.

I saw Reginald right up close, the way he'd liked to be with me, in my face. My husband and my manager, he'd dicked me over on both scores and left me high and dry before I took up the gloves again and won back the championship.

I remember when I first started training, a man said that women shouldn't fight. But I told him there was nothing wrong with us finally learning how to use our bodies and give a good right hook after all those centuries of more manipulative mental manoeuvres. I called it the Geisha Syndrome. On the exterior we appeared agreeable and polite, but inside we remained at war. That stuff's fucked us up, I told the man.

When I got the slammer in the head I saw stars and began going down on my knees, I could feel my legs folding up like a map. I saw my son, Delfi, in the audience near the ropes. He hated me fighting, but he came every time, one of the great loves of my life. When he was a baby I used to go out the back and feed him between bouts.

I saw all the money I'd made and all the money Reg had spent on my behalf. Ha! I saw Delfi on his pink cuddle blanket sucking his big moist thumb, and I saw Frank crying after he'd asked me on one knee to marry him and I'd turned him down. And Eki's soft hairless body, smooth as a brown egg; he could never stop smiling when he was drunk. In bed he'd talk about tigers, and I'd untie his hair and brush it.

I saw the six thousand nine hundred and thirty-nine dawns I'd spent up at five since Reg had first begun training me at sixteen. Reg said I'd been a scrawny thankless bitch. Thin and quiet, I'd been an orphan then for eight years. I saw the dog the Big Swede had given me, black and silky. I'd named him after my sweetest, tastiest fight in Chicago.

I saw my own mother's face the last day before the accident. She'd been smiling then, turning and waving to me as I'd gone through the school gate, quickly absorbed into the swell of human movement. I saw the ring ropes. I saw something shaped like a cloud. I was on my knees, and then on my elbows. I could hear the crowd, they were shouting 'Treasure'. That was my professional name: Treasure Maye Godiva. But for a minute it sounded like 'Pleasure', then the lights went out. I think I swore, but I can't remember anything more.

# A Piece of Yellow Soap
## FRANK SARGESON

SHE IS DEAD now, that woman who used to hold a great piece of yellow washing soap in her hand as she stood at her kitchen door. I was a milkman in those days. The woman owed a bill to the firm I worked for, and each Saturday I was expected to collect a sum that would pay for the week's milk, and pay something off the amount overdue. Well, I never collected anything at all. It was because of that piece of yellow soap.

I shall never forget those Saturday mornings. The woman had two advantages over me. She used to stand at the top of the steps and I used to stand at the bottom; and she always came out holding a piece of yellow soap. We used to argue. I would always start off by being very firm. Didn't my living depend on my getting money out of the people I served? But out of this woman I never got a penny. The more I argued the tighter the woman would curl her fingers on to the soap; and her fingers, just out of the washtub, were always bloodless and shrunken. I knew what they must have felt like to her. I didn't like getting my own fingers bloodless and shrunken. My eyes would get fixed on her fingers and the soap, and after a few minutes I would lose all power to look the woman in the face. I would mumble something to myself and take myself off.

I have often wondered whether the woman knew anything about the power her piece of yellow soap had over me, whether she used it as effectively on other tradesmen as she used it on me. I can't help feeling that she did know. Sometimes I used to pass her along the street, out of working hours. She acknowledged me only by staring at me, her eyes like pieces of rock.

She had a way too of feeling inside her handbag as she passed me, and I always had the queer feeling that she carried there a piece of soap. It was her talisman, powerful to work wonders, to create round her a circle through which the more desperate harshness of the world could never penetrate.

Well, she is dead now, that woman. If she has passed into Heaven I can't help wondering whether she passed in holding tight to a piece of yellow washing soap. I'm not sure that I believe in Heaven or God myself, but if God is a Person of Sensibility I don't doubt that when He looked at that piece of yellow washing soap He felt ashamed of Himself.

# *Taniwha Gold*
## JOY MACKENZIE

HE IS DEAD now, that young man who used to come collecting money for the milk bill. I feel kind of ashamed. Not that it was my fault. So sensitive, these young men. Well, just a boy he was actually. I reckon the milkman's lad would have been about seventeen. I was a bit rough on him, I suppose. Not that I gave him a hard time or anything like that. I didn't have the money, you see. I've got all these kids and my old man took off years ago, and I've got to have milk, don't I?

That lad, he was easy to cast a spell on. My Taniwha is just a piece of soap, but it seemed to make him uncomfortable. My hands aren't the best — all sort of wrinkled and pale on account of all the washing I do. I don't have a washing machine, you see. And with six kids there's a lot of clothes to wash. I don't mind washing. As a matter of fact, I quite like it. All those soapy suds and the nice clean smell, and it's kind of peaceful, you know? My wash-house is just off the verandah and I was always in it whenever the lad came. I'd walk out to the top of the steps with the Taniwha in my hand and just look at him.

'Come for the milk money, missus,' he'd say.

I'd be squeezing the soap and he'd be staring at the Taniwha.

'Come back next week. My old man will be back then.'

I never thought he would. Tell the truth, I never thought we'd see the old man again. The bill had been mounting up for ages and I knew I hadn't a hope of paying it off. So one day I slumped down by the concrete tub and pretended to be dead. I wouldn't've minded being an actress. You know, you have your dreams before you get married and have kids, and then that's the end of all that. Anyhow, I lay there dead quiet, and the lad came to the top of the steps. He'd never done that before. He saw me lying there by the pile of dirty washing, the tub full of soapy water. And the Taniwha. Well, that was on the floor too. Maybe he thought I'd slipped on it and bumped my head. I don't know what he thought, but the fact is, he tore down those steps, got on his bike and took off.

You wouldn't believe it but my old man chose that exact minute to come home – the rotten bastard – and he knocked the poor boy over with his truck. Now what did that lad do except try to collect his father's debts? I hope God feels ashamed of himself, killing off the innocent while my dirty rotten hubby is alive and kicking some other poor woman around by now, I shouldn't wonder. I never did pay the milk bill either.

# The Floe Riders
## BRITTA STABENOW

THE WINTER YOUNG Eskander came down to the docks, a bitter freeze turned all things brittle. No rain or snow fell. In the desiccated atmosphere doors and tempers warped, and cut flowers wilted the moment they arrived within the city walls.

No pupil from the lyceum had ever approached one of the waterside gangs before. What could any of them gain from us? Kalle wondered. He was amused at this round-cheeked boy in his fine school uniform; sending him off to fetch some pigeon's milk would be easy sport.

Ice-breakers were prowling the river. The tall spires of the merchant houses divided up the sky, and Kalle said, Aren't you the one who will take over the House of Eskander one day?

The boy replied, Please – my name is Ludovis. Will you show me how to ride?

Kalle's gang spent the daytime working the horse trams. He knew his trade; none of his boys, collecting the dung as they flitted between the carriages, was ever delivered home with crushed limbs. But the long twilight found all the gangs by the river. Sometimes they saw grown men cross over in search of food or work; they skipped from floe to floe, mindful, calculating the danger. The boys rode the floes for the unalloyed risk and joy; because it wiped away the feel of coins pressed into their palms. They knew that every winter the ice would demand its dues: someone caught in a grinding embrace between two floes, or buried beneath colliding layers that reared up like sea lions.

Kalle soon found Ludovis needed little teaching. The boy – so ungainly on land – appeared to dance his way over the floes, and he casually picked up the high-pitched sound waves of fractures racing through the ice. Kalle battled the floes, but Ludo was a seal riding with the currents.

One day, when they were watching the freighters crunching through the brash ice to the open sea, Ludovis told Kalle his secret wish; that he might get on board and travel far away from here.

Kalle gave a short, dry laugh. Hadn't they all tried to stow away! But it was impossible.

The time had come for Ludo's great test. He would cross the river and return in a straight line, and thus become a full member of the gang. They watched him glide into the dusk, spotted him against the luminous white on his way back. Kalle realised that he was gone for good the moment he saw Ludo pause in the middle of the river, then jump sideways on to a floe swirling downstream.

Old Eskander sent for Kalle and asked him, Why? But all Kalle knew was that Ludo used to beg the old sailors to tell him about the herring gloaming: how shoals upon shoals of silver would rise up from the deep and the dark midnight sea star-burst into molten light, a short-lived Milky Way across the implacable swell.

# Friday Nights
## BEN YONG

For J

SHE'S ONLY TWENTY-TWO. She says, Jesus I hate Friday nights, always expected to do something. I sip my drink. Don't you think? she asks me, shaking her glass in my direction.

When my brother was sixteen years old, my father threw a plate at his face. My brother raised his arm to protect himself, and so the plate shattered against his hand and cut open his cheek. After that he left home and my mother and I were told not to visit him. But every Friday night we did anyway. We would take the car as soon as Dad got back from work, saying we wanted to go into town. My father watched my face as my mother gave our usual explanation. Then we would drive to my brother's flat, pick him up and head into town. Often we would go to a video parlour to keep me quiet. I remember walking around, steel tokens heavy in my sweating hand, the set darkness punctuated with flashes of multicoloured light, my mother standing over my brother and me as we manoeuvred jet fighters through escalating alien onslaughts. I made my money last.

Afterwards we would go back to my brother's empty flat, where he lived alone, and my brother and Mum would talk over what had happened during the week. I listened to their talk with the sound of video games fading in my ears, waiting to go home.

I wanted to be the centre of their attention. One time, I insisted on having takeaways. They had sighed and got up, taking their coats. Stay here, my mother said, and then they left. All right, I said. I watched TV for over an hour, then began to glance at my watch every five minutes. It didn't take that long to get takeaways, I reasoned, and I began to wonder if they weren't lying somewhere, on some road, bodies broken, silent mouths gaping, my mother's arm perhaps draped like a lover's across my brother's chest, fried chicken and hamburgers and glass scattered over the road. My father answers the door and says, But where's Alex? The policemen look at each other for a moment and say, There was no one else in the car, sir.

I ring my best friend and say, They're not back yet. Where are they? I don't know where they are. He puts his mother on and she says to me, Why don't you call home? I can't, I say, he'll kill me, and at that moment I believe it. She asks, Isn't there anyone else you can call? No, I say, you're it. She is silent, and then she says, It'll be all right, just wait. At that moment they return, and their smiles turn to frowns. Who are you calling? my brother asks.

Are you all right? they ask. Mother, brother, father, prospective lover. They regard me with suspicion.

My mouth works endlessly. I cannot begin to explain what it is I want to say.

# King of the Tarseal
## PATRICIA MURPHY

HE WAS NINETEEN when his uncle lent him the money. Always easy for a touch was old Sid. Not like his dad, who wouldn't part with the pickings from his nose.

'If you want a motorbike, bloody well save for it. When I was your age . . . blah . . .blah . . .'

When he was 'his age' there were jobs, and there weren't girls with legs that went on forever. Girls in his day were younger editions of Mum – and they went on buses. You couldn't take a bird on a bus now. Try that on and they wouldn't go out with you twice. He knew.

Anyway, he was paying Sid twenty a week from the dole money, so what was all the noise about?

He bought it off a joker shifting to Aussie. Beaut job with masses of polished chrome. Colossus astride a wild stallion, he roared up the Moonshine. And no shortage of girls, either. There was a long redhead with a mouth like a ripe boysenberry. God but she was good, that one.

King of the Tarseal, she was his Queen – for a month.

Then she wanted him to trade in the bike for a car. When he refused, she dropped him for the guy from the panelbeaters. No sweat; he settled for a college girl. But she was dead scared if he went over ninety.

'Oooooh, oooooh . . . slow down, Kev. PLEASE . . . Oh God!'

He took her to the foreshore. She was dead scared there too.

'Don't ask me to go with you again,' she bawled.

'That'll be the day,' he mumbled, and left her to walk home.

The blonde from the dairy was best. Warm as buttermilk, she perched up close, pale hair streaming out from under the helmet.

'Faster . . . faster . . .' she shouted into the wind.

He laughed all the way to Paekakariki.

'Faster . . . faster . . .' she moaned as the dune sand filled her hair.

But he was on his own when the Big Mack outfit collected him. The helmet saved his head – not a bruise on his face. His dad couldn't understand it. He didn't look at the rest of him – just made the necessary arrangements.

The girl with the fruity mouth shivered. For days she talked about it to the others. 'Just think . . . if I'd still been going out with him, I might have copped it too.'

They listened, round-eyed, picturing her battered to a pulp in her fancy stitched jeans.

The family blamed Sid. After the funeral, Mum abused him. 'If it wasn't for your sodding fat wallet, our Kevin'd be alive today.'

'Right,' he cried, 'that's it. Don't none of youse ask for a helping hand. Fond of young Kev, I was. Like one of m'own.'

The blonde from the dairy went slower and slower about her work.

'Two milkshakes, Tracey . . . get a shift on, girl.'

She planted marigolds on the grave at Christmas. Come the New Year, she moved to Auckland and in the long hot summer the marigolds withered around the plastic roses.

# *Carnivore*
## ROWAN METCALFE

ONE DAY MARGARET found herself purchasing a large roasting pan, which was disturbing. She carried it home and spent some time considering the best place to secrete it, where it would be least likely to offend. In the end she decided on the cleaning cupboard, seldom opened except by herself. For her husband was a man of delicate sensibilities, a vegetarian, and the sight of a roasting pan might upset him. No flesh had passed his lips for almost twenty years. Now in his prime, he was handsome and well fed, a fine figure of a man. Some vegetarians have an ascetic appearance, but not Margaret's husband. He dined like a rajah on all manner of nuts and grains and fruits. Not abjuring dairy products, he was sleek and glossy with accumulated milk fats. He enjoyed buttery cakes with sugary icing, steaming nut roasts and fritters of twice-cooked bananas. Margaret prided herself on her cuisine.

At first she had continued to introduce small morsels of flesh into her own diet. A little sirloin browned on either side, with rosemary and a dash of cream, a moist leg of chicken with a crisp golden skin. But she had been reminded, with aggrieved reproaches and mournful insistence, that these were the decaying remains of once-living, sentient creatures, helpless to resist the slaughterer's knife. Eventually she had learned to avert her eyes as she passed the meat counter, lest her bloodlust return. But lately she had found herself lingering there again, gazing at a tray of glistening kidneys, or a whole Italian salami looped up on a string. She had helped herself to several toothpicked samples of honey-roasted ham one day, and had to come home and clean her teeth thoroughly lest it be detected. Now the roasting pan.

When he came in at the end of the day, she offered, as often, to massage him. He lay down obediently, she unbuckled his belt, unbuttoned his shirt and rubbed her hands with oil. He sighed with pleasure as she ran her palms up his flanks. She loved to feel the melting contours of muscle beneath his fine skin, the soft layer of flesh that eluded her pinch, the invisible silky coating of his bones. She loved the little furred pocket of fat on his belly that warmed the small of her back at night, the clean milky smell of him. Her fingers closed around the soft tabs of his hips, she closed her eyes, and, remembering all of a sudden the roasting pan, saw herself drawing from the oven a rack of dainty ribs sizzling in their own buttery sweet fat, with a hint of cashew and kumara to the aroma, a suggestion of fresh herbs. Her mouth flushed with saliva and, before she knew it, she was wondering whether a medium white, or a soft, fruity red . . .

'Penny for your thoughts, darling,' he said. But she only smiled, and gazed at him tenderly.

# Two Down
## CHRIS ELSE

THE CROSSWORD WAS a cryptic. I was doing pretty well with it except for the upper left-hand corner. There was one word there that really had me. It seemed so obvious, and yet the obvious was impossible. Finally I asked Wendy. I knew she wouldn't know the answer. She hates crosswords.

'Fast,' I said.

'What?' She looked up from her knitting.

'Five letters meaning fast. Ends in K.'

'Quick,' she said. I knew she'd say that.

'But if two down's 'quick', then one across ends in Q. Doesn't work.'

'Don't ask me,' she said. 'I wouldn't have a clue.'

Suddenly, sitting there, I had a strange sensation. I could hear everything. There was the clock ticking and the little clicks from Wendy's needle tips and the soft patter of the rain outside. There was a dog barking somewhere and the traffic on the road and strange little cracks and creakings from the house. There was my breathing, I could hear it, going in and out, and the rustle of the newspaper in my hands. I looked across at Wendy. She was sitting with her back to the window, and the light made a fine silver halo of her hair. Her face was in shadow, head tilted to the left. The two round discs of her glasses gleamed.

I didn't know what to do. I stood up and the springs in my chair began to spang and sing. I walked over to the window. The rain was dripping, spattering, pocking on the path and on the hedge and on the vegetables.

And then I saw it. Big. Right there, standing in the rows of lettuces. It was a bird, the size of a goose. Its body and wings and legs and neck were all a soft, deep pink, like strawberry ice-cream. Its head was brown, dark chocolate, and its bill blunt and rounded, sloping in the same curve as the slope of its skull so that the whole of its head looked like a basin upside down. I couldn't see its eyes in the dark feathers, but just below where they might have been, along its cheek, there were five little gold rings in a wavy line.

'Hey,' I said, turning to Wendy. 'Come and look at this.'

'What?' She didn't move.

'This bird. What is it?'

She twisted in her chair, pushed her glasses up her nose, and stared into the garden.

'It's a sparrow,' she said.

I looked back out again. The goose had gone. There was a sparrow there, though, hopping along in the dirt.

I stared at it, wondering. The clock went on ticking, just as loud. And what can you do, really? I mean, how can one across end in Q? It doesn't make sense.

# Ton-up
## BERNARD BROWN

WHEN I LIVED in Pareora as a kid, the only excitement was the weekly discharge of freezing works offal into the sea. Red Friday. That is, until Jessie and Vernon did their thing on the motorbike.

Vern had bought the old machine from someone at Knickknacks. It had so many bits and pieces from other bikes that it took on an identity all its own. And it could travel. Boy, how it could move.

Jessie, Knickknacks' girl, was older and bigger than him and quite hard-minded. Some said she'd set her sights on the bike rather than Vern. But she had to coax him up to get a ride. What she most desired and finally got was an up-front.

It was a bitterly cold night. The night after Norm Kirk had made his election pitch at Palmerston North about locking bikies up. Vern had at last given way to Jessie's pleas to drive it ('Do a quick ton or two,' as she put it) up the back road behind the Works.

There was no one much to disturb there. Only one house – a dilapidated shed of a place where a crummy collection of brothers named Scroggs lived. All bachelors and looking like they'd come out of *Cold Comfort Farm*. Really thick and scruffy. The main attraction for bikers was a humpback bridge a couple of paddocks up the track from the Scroggses, where – at the right speed – you could do a real flier. Vern had treated me to it once and I never forgot it.

As I say, on this night it was biting cold. After a first run on the flat Jessie told Vern they needed to put their overcoats on, back to front to keep the wind out of their chests. And they went around the back of each other to do up their buttons.

Jessie then took off. With him riding pillion. No one knows

exactly what happened, but the story has it that she was a couple of miles past the humpback and feeling real high when she sensed Vern wasn't any longer on the bike. She turned and raced back, and there, on the bridge, were the Scroggses. Standing around a body.

It was Vern. 'Vern! Vern!' she screeched. 'What's happened to you?'

Vern, in no shape to respond, stayed prone. One of the older Scroggses, shuffling a bit, looked over to her. 'We done what we could, gal,' he said. 'When youse went over the hump he musta come off. When we got here he was layin' on the track makin' a helluva noise. Fred here and me, we saw that somethink was wrong. So we jerked his head round so's it faced the right way.' He looked down at the figure of Vern, still utterly prone. 'And we haven't had a bloody word out've 'im since.'

# *Aubade*
## OWEN MARSHALL

THE JUSTICE DEPARTMENT Hostel was as all hostels, as all institutions which are held in common and by an unwilling and transient population. It declared itself by signs of piecemeal maintenance and general, inexorable decay. It was grey like the enamel of an old tooth; the strip of cloud in the still, early morning was the same grey. How exact and unremarkable it all was, she thought; how difficult to shake off. Nothing moved, lest it become a target for the watching chill of dawn. Nothing moved, for a movement would begin the day. Jessop had it coming though, no doubt about that, she thought. She remembered how far his face tipped back when it was over.

To the right of the high window ledge was the flat roof of the service area, with the aluminium sheeting in raised strips. Patterns of dust and fine debris had formed, and there was a pink sweatshirt which had been lying there for a long time, for it was much faded and set in rigid folds like the skin of an animal long dead by the roadside. Jessop was still somewhere though, wasn't he, despite what she'd been told? He'd often said that it would take more than a mean slut like her to put him down. A stiff drag and the weed was at its job. The smoke hung as a mist in the still air.

Concrete sides and older wooden sides of the building were at all angles, and above the strip roofing of the service block a long board had been fastened between the side of her building and the next, and on it were fastened a pipe and wires, like a lifeline. Birds had found it a pleasant perch, and on the roof below, mimicking its course, was a line of chalky droppings. On the high buildings the paint had cracked from the bargeboards, particularly at the corners where the moisture was able to get in, and a mildew-like mustard flourished. On the old wood of the nearest corner a new spotlight for the quad had been fitted. Its outer case was of bright green aluminium, as if a single leaf bud had burst from the whole warped length of that wooden stem. Once perhaps she had loved Jessop, or wanted him anyway: the inverted pyramid of his torso, wide in the shoulders, a sharp point at the loins. Yes indeed. In the firelight the flat of his chest had often been a table for two glasses and their fish and chips.

An amazing number and variety of snorkels rose through the roof: thick chimneys, round ventilator ducts with conical tin hats, lavatory vents with archaic, wire bulbs at the top like the little traps in which yellow soap used to be shaken in the sink. And hot water overflows; delicate reeds among the other fixtures. The roofs showed so much more sign of life than she had ever realised, whereas it was the sides of the buildings that were barren. Just cliffs of uniform descent, with only windows as a break, all closed and all in rank and file. While on the roof tufts of grass could be seen above the gutterings, and TV aerials were the hieroglyphics of the new world. A forest up there, she thought. Jessop's last emotion she was sure was surprise, rather than fear or anger. Surprise that after all she could start his blood flowing, and he couldn't staunch it. Surprise, amazement even, that he was not going to teach her a lesson as he always had before.

She had supposed that at the end it would be just a general image; vaguely realised buildings and sky, yet definition remained exact. Rather, the inner world was a flux, and the irrelevance around her had the detail of a footprint, the authenticity of the sky's cold sheen. She was cold on the ledge; goose pimples and hairs stood up on her pale arm. Her fingers whitened in their grip on the frame, and beside her thumb with its peeping moon of cuticle, a rust stain through both putty and paint gave away the hidden head of a nail. The blue leather of her sneakers picked up an odd dust weathered from the ledge, and when she began to fall she took her breath with a gasp because the air was suddenly colder, as if it had all at once begun to blow, instead of hers being the rush against it.

# Coals of Fire
## MARY STUART

HAD I BEEN able to get out of bed, I would have cheerfully strangled her. Never had I heard such continuous snoring. Within two minutes of her putting off her light, it would start, a steady rumbling sound, rising to a crescendo that reverberated throughout the room like the first rumblings of a volcano. I tried everything: earplugs, the radio playing softly, coughing discreetly, then not so discreetly. All to no avail. The terrible noise continued with little or no let-up the whole night long.

For three nights, what with the pain in my legs and Mrs Brown's molten rumblings, I hardly slept. I could bear it no longer; I asked the night nurse if I could be moved. Next night when it was time for us to go to sleep, I was told they were going to move Mrs Brown, not me, as others in the ward were also being disturbed. What a relief. But when the nurse asked her if she minded going to another room for the night, the great whale of a woman started to cry.

'Why, what have I done?' she whimpered, while the nurse whispered something I couldn't hear. I began to wish I'd never said a word. I lay there, my heart racing – it was all I could do not to call out that I was sorry to have upset her and was sure it would be better tonight. I kept silent, however, and went on pulling a mandarin to pieces slowly and methodically.

Later that night a nurse helped me to the lavatory, my first time out of bed, telling me to ring the bell when I was ready to go back. I rang and rang, then opened the door and called out. A large figure hove into sight. 'Take my arm,' Mrs Brown said as she gently helped me back to bed.

# *Butterflies*
## PATRICIA GRACE

THE GRANDMOTHER PLAITED her granddaughter's hair and then she said, 'Get your lunch. Put it in your bag. Get your apple. You come back straight after school, straight home here. Listen to the teacher,' she said. 'Do what she say.'

Her grandfather was out on the step. He walked down the path with her and out on to the footpath. He said to a neighbour, 'Our granddaughter goes to school. She lives with us now.'

'She's fine,' the neighbour said. 'She's terrific with her two plaits in her hair.'

'And clever,' the grandfather said. 'Writes every day in her book.'

'She's fine,' the neighbour said.

The grandfather waited with his granddaughter by the crossing and then he said, 'Go to school. Listen to the teacher. Do what she say.'

When the granddaughter came home from school her grandfather was hoeing round the cabbages. Her grandmother was picking beans. They stopped their work.

'You bring your book home?' the grandmother asked.

'Yes.'

'You write your story?'

'Yes.'

'What's your story?'

'About the butterflies.'

'Get your book, then. Read your story.'

The granddaughter took her book from her schoolbag and opened it.

'I killed all the butterflies,' she read. 'This is me and this is all the butterflies.'

'And your teacher like your story, did she?'

'I don't know.'

'What your teacher say?'

'She said butterflies are beautiful creatures. They hatch out and fly in the sun. The butterflies visit all the pretty flowers, she said. They lay their eggs and then they die. You don't kill butterflies, that's what she said.'

The grandmother and grandfather were quiet for a long time, and their granddaughter, holding the book, stood quite still in the warm garden.

'Because you see,' the grandfather said, 'your teacher, she buy all her cabbages from the supermarket and that's why.'

# just another wednesday night on the west coast waiting for the muse to strike
## SARAH QUIGLEY

it's 4 am and the sun's licking the back of my neck which
makes me a bit uncomfortable but i know i'm on a mission i think
i might just catch the big one and i hear a voice coming over my
shoulder
— may-ate it says and there's keri hulme in a ball dress
— mate she says how the hell are ya and what are ya doing
— i'm fishing i say
— what for she says
— for words i say
— prose or the other she says
— the other i say and i say it loudly because i know in my bones
i'll be hooking up genius any minute now
— ya could be waiting a while says keri come back for a cuppa
i've got plenty of words for the taking she says i chopped up the
bone people and never used them since

so we go to her hut just a little hut and it's leaning out way over
the sea
— got a few mates in to hear you read she says
and i look round and there's margaret mahy sinking a home brew
there's brian turner and owen marshall and stevan double-barrelled
grigg eating whitebait patties and there's janet frame just lighting
up the room with her big hair

— all mainlanders ya see says keri cos we hafta stick together

just then katherine mansfield walks in late
— what's she doing here I say and i start to feel nervous
— wouldn't miss it she says she has a wellington accent and
london clothes and it puts me off in a major way

i look around for my words i know they're somewhere but i
can't remember where i'm starting to sweat km rolls a joint steve
and owen play drinking games janet just looks rapt
— start small says keri
— like a mental midget says km

black rage hot as hell thick as mud boils up in my head
— back in a minute i say that's what i say and i walk out the door
and over the cliff
— arohanui mate i hear keri cry as i go

i fly like a god and i eagle-eye for my poem
the sea's below me and then there's the beach and there's my
masterpiece stretched out on the sand
and i dive towards it to get the first word
it starts with an L or maybe an A
well no it's a 4 and then there's a
ok it's a 4 so that's no big deal and what looks like a 5 yes i see
it's a 5
and then there's a 9 a big fucken 9 so it's 4.59 written out on
the sand it's 4.59 in the bloody am
i can't see my words because of the dark i can't hear my words
because of the snoring

so it's 5 am don't they always say that's the darkest hour

# *Fax*
## JOHN CONNOR

Dear Darling,

Please forgive me, sir, for calling you darling. It won't happen again, I promise. I'm afraid I might be showing signs of the peculiar malady which has come to my attention lately. I hope this fax arrives at your office in time for you to marshal whatever resources are necessary. Drastic measures must be taken; I'm convinced of that, and I know how drastic your measures can be. Your recent eradication of pathological dissatisfaction amongst us, by low-level aerial spraying, was exemplary, if I may say so. This particular malady unfortunately, if not stopped, will destroy our well-ordered society more certainly than pathological dissatisfaction ever could.

The other day, at the bus stop outside my office, a man, an otherwise perfectly normal and satisfied man, bit another man on the finger as the other man raised his hand to signal a bus; bit him then ran off tittering to himself.

Well, darling. How are your buttocks today? Plenty of spots on them I hope. I like buttocks with plenty of spots on them. They remind me so much of the wonderful steamed raisin puddings my mother used to make. I'm sorry, sir. Please forgive me. I'd erase what I've just written if I weren't so terrified of being overwhelmed and unable to continue. Yesterday at a very important lunchtime meeting of dignitaries, functionaries and leading government officials, one of the invited guests rose as if to speak but, instead turned, bent over and emitted a loud, trouser-ripping fart which set the crystal glassware ringing. While everyone reeled back gasping and rubbing their eyes he ran off tittering to himself. At dinner that same evening a normally polite and well-behaved boy lined up the peas on the edge of his plate and, raising the plate to firing level, flicked each pea, one at a time, at his poor mother sitting opposite, the last few landing straight into her wide open mouth. After he'd finished, the boy merely tittered to himself and asked if there was any steamed raisin pudding for dessert.

One of my colleagues has suggested this malady is a bizarre manifestation of unconscious rebellion against a stern and cruel father. He's very glib, this colleague, with a tipped-up bowl of minestrone soup dripping through his hair and beard he's very glib and laughable. I laughed at him. What rubbish. I never had a father, stern, cruel or otherwise, and I have dedicated my life to furthering the enlightened and benevolent policies of people such as yourself, Sir, you lovable overinflated pig's bladder. What is there to rebel against? Perhaps my colleague's other theory is right. The low-level aerial spraying has affected certain sensitive people's biochemistry and resulted in this strange outbreak. I look forward to your arrival with the antidote, but I must warn you, I have sharpened the plastic spoon's handle to a point and won't hesitate to use it.

Yours et cetera

# Is Raining Soon
## MICHAEL MORRISSEY

WHENEVER I PLAY something mildly classical –Tchaikovsky or Strauss – the door bursts open and my mother sweeps into the room. She will spin several turns of some old-time waltz, dancing as though held by a partner, my father perhaps, though probably not, as I never saw him move his feet except under the compulsion of some practical task – leaving for work, going outside to chop firewood or roll the lawn level though it is as flat as human endeavour can make it.

My mother, who has an unadventurously compact figure, had once been serious about her dancing – not a professional but dedicated enough to win several cups in fiercely competitive ballroom dance-offs. On occasion these shallow chalices have done time as egg cups. Wistfully she will remark that when she married she stopped going to dances. Marriage was the end of the dancing but, as documents will prove, the beginning of my existence.

Last week my father got the call from the great dancer in the sky.

That was the recent past.

This is the present: I come home and find my mother dancing with a very tall black man. She is smiling, he is grave. As my father has only been dead an indecently short time, I am mindful of the severity of Hamlet's remarks to his mother, but tastefully do not repeat them. The music is not Strauss; Victor Silvester perhaps, or even Glenn Miller.

There is a shocking amount of loose social energy in the room. The rapidly overheating couple detach into the short white figure of my mother, her face joyously and guiltlessly flushed, and the silent tall grave black man.

'This is Ahmed,' she says. 'He does not speak English.'

I hullo Ahmed nevertheless and, whether out of polite imitation or because my mother has erred in her estimation of his linguistic abilities, he says hello back. Our dialogue apparently at an end, their dancing continues. Their confidence makes me unsure of my next action, which turns out to be sitting down and reading, or pretending to, the newspaper, which is replete with newspapery things like a mother butchering her children because there was no food in the refrigerator. I consider butchering Ahmed for holding my mother in that presumptuous silent way, but protected by the invisible force of old-time waltzing, he is immune to hostile thoughts.

At last the dancers truly separate and my mother says Ahmed was delivering some pamphlets, bargains at a nearby supermarket perhaps, when they struck up a conversation, which seems to contradict his not having English. Past withered old curtains that washing can only destroy, the sun is blazing in a blue blue sky and Ahmed's teeth are blazing, for he is smiling at my mother and at me.

'Is raining soon,' he says.

# *Jock*
## RACHAEL KING

JOCK LIVED IN a huge bare warehouse in the middle of town. In winter his breath hung in the air like ice. To keep warm he made alcohol. Sometimes he branched out into cinnamon alcohol or blackberry alcohol, but mostly it was brown alcohol and white alcohol. We would come around to help him drink each new batch. We got drunk, but none as drunk as Jock, because he was fearless when it came to his own drink. The night that Jock held light in the palm of his hand, as Robin remembered it, Stacy left Jock. Jock didn't remember it at all. He just woke up the next day, shivering, his hand in a bowl of ice. The ice didn't stand a chance of melting in that room, not on that morning. Blisters and pink raw skin. His stomach sick to touch.

He had been showing off the potency of his drink. The white alcohol. Started by burning it on a silver tray that became too hot to hold. Blue flame licking it. Then he got bold and poured it on his hand and lit that. He didn't feel the pain until it was too late, but he kept quiet. Wouldn't let on that as soon as we all left he would open the window and scream. For a brief moment he had a look of total serenity on his face as we watched the fire move around his palm, between his fingers. This was when Robin woke up from the couch and saw it, the light, and his face. She went back to sleep, smiling. And this was when Stacy knew that Jock had gone too far this time and that she would leave with everyone else that night. Just when she knew he would be in pain and would need her the most.

So the next morning Jock was just sitting there staring at his hand and wondering what had happened, when Robin arrived with coffee and fresh bagels and a glow to her cheeks he hadn't noticed before. Stacy gave her blessing and now it's summer and the warehouse isn't so cold.

# Useless Flesh
## ROGER HALL

IT WAS A long time ago.

The campus graffiti was pale now, but to him it stood out like fresh day-glo: 'A woman needs a man like a fish needs a bicycle.'

Lorna had laughed, but he'd been offended.

'Men have taken away the night from us.'

Yes, yes, he could see that was fair. But not the joke that Lorna came home with one day:

'What's the useless piece of flesh at the end of a penis called?' 'A man.' Clever. Yes. Funny? Yes. But . . . wasn't it all getting a bit much?

He applied them all as a sort of check list to himself: Good with the kids? Yes. Housework? Could do better. Attitude to women? Surely okay. Useless? No, not useless.

He knew how women must feel at night, that *of course* men must seem a threat. If a woman was walking along the street towards him, he would often cross the road deliberately, so she wouldn't have anything to fear. He wanted to call out, 'It's okay. You're safe. I'm harmless.'

Lorna had gone. A new job. Up north. Taken the kids. He'd tried commuting, but it didn't work out. She seemed content on her own. What was it he'd done wrong? What was it she *wanted*?

You couldn't even offer anyone a ride these days. In his first years, passing a bus stop he'd pick up students, neighbours of either gender. Nothing stupid. Not a kid. Not a woman. A male student, why not? But now . . . look straight ahead, drive on.

He missed the kids. Bath-time. Reading at night. It was supposed to be a duty, but the books were great; colourful, funny. They'd gone from *Where's Lowly Worm?* to sophisticated jokes. What were they reading now?

He compensated in the usual way. Worked longer and longer hours. Drove late to his one-bedroom flat. Didn't bother to cook. Recently the first transition. Worked late, then change into running gear. He would run ten, now it was twenty minutes before going home.

He looked at himself in the mirror. *Crimewatch* would have described him as: 'Caucasian male, five feet eleven, late thirties, short brown hair, no distinguishing features . . .' With tracksuit and sneakers, he could well be setting out for a bit of bother: a petrol station perhaps? A dairy? Hideous thought: campus rapist.

He ran. The glow was more virtue than physical. Arrived back at his car, parked by the shrubs intended to beautify the place. A young woman was putting a leaflet under his windscreen wiper. She gasped at his arrival, started to back away.

'Hi,' he said pleasantly.

She backed away from him as if he were a snake. He moved forward a step.

'Listen. It's okay.'

She turned away, fearful.

He took two quick steps and grabbed her by the arm.

'It's *okay*,' he stressed. 'I won't hurt you.'

She went limp, sliding down. It was intensely irritating. Before she reached the ground, he was hitting her.

# Pushing Up Daisies
## NOEL SIMPSON

ON ONE OF my rare visits to the rest home Dad rebuked me for not keeping in touch with my only brother, Jack. 'You must keep in touch,' he said. 'This time next year I'll be pushing up daisies.' Dad was eighty-three and had recently lost his wife, his home and his best friend. Poor old bastard. 'Oh yes,' I said, 'okay, we'll keep in touch. I saw Jack last month. I'll send him a card for his birthday as well as at Christmas time. What are the meals like here, Dad?'

Oh yes, better to ignore remarks like that. *I'll be pushing up daisies.* How embarrassing! I didn't want to talk about it. But as casual as that! *I'll be pushing up daisies.* He could have said, 'This time next year I'll be ashes,' or, 'This time next year I'll be six feet under.'

Like saying it about old Joe Bloggs, the guy across the road. 'This time next year Bloggsie will be pushing up daisies.'

He said I was to have his barometer and his outdoor bowls. My brother Jack had been given plenty of things and was not to have those. He . . . absolutely . . . insisted . . . I was to have . . . the barometer and the bowls. He wasn't a bad old bastard.

According to the doctor there was nothing seriously the matter with Dad. Yes, yes, he was going downhill. But there was no cancer. Nothing terminal. My brother said Dad was fine, just a great worrier. Silly old bastard.

My wife, Kate, was Dad's favourite. 'My daughter,' he would say proudly, beaming, because he hadn't any daughters of his own and he loved her like a daughter. He was a nice old bastard.

'I can see him slipping away before my eyes,' said the doctor eight months later. 'Yet I can't find anything wrong with him. He's had all the tests. He's not in pain.'

He died suddenly, well sort of suddenly, a month or so before he was expected to, just ten months after his horticultural forecast. He was always so punctual.

A post-mortem was done. The death certificate said 'Cardiometric Terminus'. Well of all the crazy, idiotic . . . all that means is the heart stopped beating. It always does when you die. So even the pathologist couldn't diagnose it. Or couldn't be bothered.

My wife says he simply died of a broken heart. Poor old bastard.

# Roses
## SARAH GAITANOS

ANNA NEARLY LOST her nerve at the cottage gate. Fit for her age but breathless from the climb, she didn't feel cool enough to meet Lana Leverit, and looking back down the hill she thought of free-wheeling home without further ado. Still, she was not one to quit, so she propped her bike against the picket fence, mopped her brow, then straight up the garden path she strode, through the trellis archway with the climbing rose, her eyes fixed on the yellow door. She rang the bell, waited, was about to ring again when she heard steps approaching. Breathe deeply, she told herself. Feet flat on the ground, head high, don't flinch. She'd gone through this in her mind countless times.

A slender young woman, pert as a pixie, opened the door. She was barefoot, wearing a short satin robe with a forget-me-not print the same blue as her eyes, and looked and smelt as though she'd just stepped from her shower. She hadn't dried her neck, Anna noticed.

'I'm Anna,' she began in a measured voice. The blue eyes widened. 'Anna Gibson. Bernard's wife.' She drove her look home. The girl – she was scarcely more – remained speechless. 'Ah . . . you must be Lana?'

Lana Leverit wasn't going to admit to anything, it seemed. She looked like a rabbit trapped in spotlights. Anna glanced past her into a cheerful room. She was about to ask if she could come in, but Lana, on being released from her gaze, retreated behind the door and closed it fast.

Anna waited. Had she been so intimidating?

'I just thought we'd meet,' she called through the closed door. No response. 'I don't mean you any harm.'

She really didn't, though Bernard had told her that he and Lana wished to marry. Anna, though, simply wished to exorcise her own demons. She'd never confronted his other lovers. She needed a face.

And she had one, she'd done it. As meetings went – well, it hardly rated, but she could get on now. She almost pitied the lass, way in over her depth with Bernard.

Turning her back on the yellow door, Anna heard muffled laughter from within, a deep belly laugh, not quite stifled. She knew that belly, those loose lips, that guffaw. After some eternal moments, she too could see the humour.

There was a light scent in the air from the climbing rose where small creamy blooms tumbled over the trellis like a mantle for a bride. Anna imagined herself wrapping it over Lana Leverit's tender shoulders, around her soft young neck, winding it tighter until the pale petals stained red.

For Bernard, though, she allowed her fantasy more satisfaction. When she had well and truly trussed him up, leaving no parts unbound, she'd deliver him like a bouquet to his bride.

Something in the way Anna walked back down the path alarmed the lovers at the window and induced a wolf whistle from an onlooker beyond the gate.

# An Expatriate Parcel of Nostalgia
## JONATHAN OWEN

Dear Son,

With you away in your remote outpost, Christmas just won't be the same, so here's a parcel of goodies to remind you of home.

The AA sign from Cape Reinga, pointing to Bluff; a fly-ridden longdrop; Mother's compost heap; a bottle of Rotorua air; a sack of Ruapehu ash; a cicada husk; a possum (with tyre marks); a hillside of manuka; a koru unfurling; a Milford Sound sandfly bite; breath-taking scenery – with power lines; lazy Sundays – and neighbourhood lawn-mowers roaring; a bach; one jandal (strap broken); pipis over a driftwood fire; a scorching ironsand beach; humming bees in red-blossomed pohutukawas blending with breaking surf; a dusty metal road – and parched throat; pub full of laughter and dark faces singing 'Ten Guitars'; black unwashed singlet (from its usual spot under your old bed); copies of *A Good Keen Man* and *Footrot Flats*; a Swanndri; a pair of well-worn tramping boots (and ripe socks); a pair of long-johns (crutch optional); an Eden Park haka; a six o'clock swill; a full chilly bin; a bottle of Bakano; cheddar chunk on cotton-wool white bread; slices of 'original recipe' Vogel; hokey-pokey ice cream and a Trumpet – minus wrapper thrown out the car window; a Waitangi Day traffic jam; a warrant of fitness (expired); Saturday night drag-races down Main Street; a waft of onion rings sizzling on someone else's barbecue; mouthfuls of hangi kumara; slice of pav; packet of Girl Guide biscuits (minus edges nibbled off by your sister); Mealmates thick with Vegemite; bag of Minties; Jaffas rolling down the aisles; Gran's pikelets with home-made jam and cream; Edmonds Cookery Book; a yellow-eyed penguin (potato chips underarm); a recording of native birdcalls introducing the morning news; a wooden Buzzy Bee; a plastic tiki; a can of She's Right attitude oil; a Red Band Taihape gumboot; a shearing gang (with smoko and scones); barbed wire with wool tufts attached; gullies of gorse; a weekend's trailer-load of rubbish; an L&P bottle; Ponsonby cappuccino — with frothy moustache; episodes from Shortland Street (and latest Anchor-family advert); old edition of the Listener; KM's short stories and James K's poems; samples of modern writing — on tagged concrete wall; an IR5 tax return; a first-past political post; a winebox enquiry; a smooth Cook Strait crossing; an audio tape of friends singing 'Now is the Hour'; sound effects of seagulls and foghorns echoing as the ship casts off; a wet handkerchief with Mother's initials; a 2½-cent stamp on postcard from our honeymoon; a playcentre white-elephant stall; your childhood photo album; your sports trophies — endlessly polished by Mother; hundreds-and-thousands sandwiches; cheerios; a red mailbox; a red coin-operated telephone box; a one-dollar note; a wharf strike; a freezing worker; a good day's fishing; a glass milk bottle; stained cuppa from the Main Trunk Line tearooms; an Anzac parade; old memories.

It's not such a bad country, is it? Take care, son. Show 'em what real Kiwis are made of, eh!

Dad

# The Lassie from Lancashire
## FRANCES CHERRY

SHE SITS IN that chair staring at her knees, she is on her soapbox again, the workers must take over the means of production, racing through a swirling past of political meetings, friends, neighbours and comrades. Dad there, young and handsome - 'people never understood what he saw in me'.

She and Dad sitting in their chairs beside each other, that's how I remember them. She reading the paper to him while he presses tobacco into his pipe, flecks falling onto his trousers and around his slippers. Her slamming the paper on to her lap, digging her fingers into her scalp. 'If I had my way I'd line them all against a wall and shoot them.'

I look at her thin bony hands, the wedding ring loose on her finger. Her watch swings around her wrist like a bracelet. She used to be such a buxom woman, breasts warm and soft to a child's head. Now there is nothing there. Even her teeth move in her mouth when she speaks. My mother is disappearing.

'Apart from your own home, this couldn't be a better place,' she says. 'They give me breakfast in bed every morning. Toast, porridge. They're very good. And of course I'm very good to them. The woman in the next room,' she gestures with her head, 'I keep an eye on her when the matron goes out, get her back into bed when she falls out. I must save them thousands of dollars.'

'That's great, Mum.'

'Did I tell you the Duchess of York came to see me?'

'No, Mum.' I look at her in surprise.

Do you know,' she looks at me intently, 'she didn't know the song

"The Grand Old Duke of York"? So I sang it and her secretary wrote it down.' She smiles down at her knees again. 'Paul's building me a house,' she says. 'He's a millionaire, you know, lives in France.'

'I don't think so, Mum.'

'Oh yes he is. He told me.'

'The last time I saw him, he lived in Sydney.'

'Well he doesn't now.' She looks up at me, her beady eyes defying me to disagree.

'Is that so?'

'He's always liked me, always kept in touch. Your father's nephew, but he's always kept in touch with me.'

'How will you live in this house? Who will look after you?'

'There'll be servants, of course.' She looks at me as if I am an imbecile. I notice that the glasses hanging around her neck are caked with food.

'A man half my age,' she says, 'wanted to marry me. I didn't trust him when his daughter brought him to see me, so I had my lawyer here as well.'

'Why was that, Mum?'

'He's started a chain of fish and chip shops,' she says indignantly. 'Wanted my secret recipe.'

'I don't want to die,' she says. 'I don't want to be nothing.'

I look at my ankles and think of her ankles. I wear her wedding ring and her old red dressing gown.

# *Warmth*
## TAMZIN BLAIR

I SHOVE IN sheets, winding them loosely around the agitator. Patting everything down, I look down at myself, at my top. Down the V-neck I can see the white lace of bra, the curve of breasts. The top needs a wash, I decide. Quickly, off with the cardy. Coldness. Pulling at cream V-necked cotton top. Pulling, brushing skin, curving warmth. Me. Bare skin, warm soft. Coming from me. From me?

Who gave it to me? This warmth.

His is different. Smooth, straight, long. When I hop into bed naked, cold.

'Cold bum, cold tits,' he jokes as I snuggle in.

Into straight, long warmth, from him to me. Not curving waves. But straight, like 'Here I am.' Mmm, nice warmth.

Hers, it's more like hers. My best friend's, when we would top'n'tail, share her-my single bed. Curving warmth, soft. I miss that warmth sometimes.

We were home alone. Someone had jumped in my bedroom window the day before. Left a crusty shoe mark of dirt on my pillow case. I had to leave it till the police came.

Listening to noises, my eyes wide, staring at my window. In the darkness, I crept to her room. Afraid, like when we were little. She lifted up the blankets. Warmth. Beside her, snuggled up, I put my arm around my sister. On a small curving waist. Softness, littleness. Curving warmth. So this is something of what I feel like, I thought.

Can't forget Mum, who is all curves and warmth. But it's so obvious. Curving warmth.

I watched her when I was little. Stroked that little curving dent above her bottom. I have one too. Watched her from their double bed. Naked, sprinkling powder – behind, floating in the air – in front, on curving tummy, soft boobs.

Mum, her warmth was there, in every child moment. Mum, in her name – Mum.

Mary-Anne. The lady from down the road. Because it's there in her too. I'd thought of it, feeling sad, feeling sad and wanting to tell her how I felt when I was young. Because she was having a hysterectomy and I thought she needed to know. But I didn't have the words or the social space. I wanted to tell her how, when I cried and she gathered me to her curving niceness, I felt warmth.

Pressed hard, not being able to breathe for boob. I liked that warmth. I wanted to tell her that what was there would always be there. That warmth.

I quickly put my cardy back on. Hugging it to me. Wool rubbing bare skin. As I'm sprinkling green washing powder, I decide I'll write a poem, a story. I'll send it to Mary-Anne.

How will I end it . . . ?

Who gave it to me? This warmth. There never was a moment when it was not.

# The Big Game
## JENNI-LYNNE HARRIS

THE CROWD WAS working itself into a frenzy. Only ten minutes to go and still the score was tied. The atmosphere was charged with tension, both on and off the field. The referee was doing all he could to keep the game from deteriorating into a full-on brawl. It's like this every year, mused George. Which was understandable. After all, this was The Shield match and both teams wanted The Log of Wood so badly.

When George first came to New Zealand he was warned about the nation's obsession with the game of rugby. Fanaticism even. But it didn't worry him. In fact, in many ways it made him feel like he was back home in Liverpool. Now that was crowd frenzy for you! It made rugby matches look tame. George missed the singing and chanting, which Kiwis seemed reluctant to embrace, but he still enjoyed the feeling of being in a big crowd, urging a team on to give its all.

Suddenly, cheering erupted as a pass by the opposition went astray and was intercepted by a red jersey. A short burst, followed by a quick flick out to the wing, and it looked as if a try was a certainty. But just ten metres out from the tryline the winger was taken in a brilliant flying tackle and the ball went into touch. The opposition won the ball from the lineout and regained twenty metres before a player was dropped in a tackle and the physio was called on. Both captains called their teams aside and desperate words were spoken. The injured player recovered and the game continued. The crowd yelled itself hoarse. Then, seemingly from out of nowhere, one of the opposition players scooped up a loose ball and charged for the line. Two red jerseys dived at the same time. There was a tense hush as all eyes went to the referee. The whistle blew and . . . 'Held up!' he called. Sighs of relief and disappointment filled the air. No victory dances yet. George looked at his watch. Only two minutes to go. 'Come on, red!' he yelled, sensing that The Shield would be heading north once again.

Fulltime, score tied. Into injury time. A lineout. Red ball. Great take and tip out. A long pass to the number 8 and the home crowd holds its breath in disbelief. The ref's arm goes up. The drop goal is over! The referee signals fulltime and the field becomes a sea of people.

George searched for the number 8 and gave him a great bear hug. 'Brilliant. Just brilliant,' he gushed. 'Aw, Dad,' said the embarrassed teenager. 'I just remembered Zinny's last droppy and I thought, if he can do it, I can give it a go too.'

'Thanks to you, The Shield's staying here this year, son. Go and get your prize.'

And as George watched him go, his heart swelled with pride. Obsession? Maybe. But this was worth it.

## Solid Matter
## KATH BEATTIE

SHE SPEEDS PAST, her shopping list a piccolo sound floating down the aisle.

'Sausages, I need sausages. Bread. Two loaves. Detergent.' She spies the fruit. 'Aaaah! Nectarines!'

I pretend I haven't heard and earnestly examine rows of canned beans and tomato sauce, trying to control the fear twinging in my soul. The voice follows. 'Sugar, raisins, condensed milk.'

My mouth dries, my neck dampens, the panic swells. Is it possible that my thoughts, too, have materialised into spoken words, intruded into personal spaces and stolen attention? How would I know? Would I hear myself? Grin and pardon myself? Would that student guffaw? That businessman frown? And that young thing with the baby, would she reply? 'Yeah, I need coffee too.'

Alarm flares. The terror. Terror that, without my knowledge, gremlins of unedited thoughts may be escaping into the atmosphere as solid matter. I can picture these phrases bouncing around the supermarket like kids on a trampoline.

. . . My neighbour is a cross-dresser . . . Aunty Margaret's become incontinent . . . Felix has fleas . . . that man's toupee is too thick . . . kiwifruit remind me of Gerald's balls . . .

My heart lurches.

What are we all doing here, anyway? No one converses. A rare nod of recognition, the inevitable 'Have a happy day' farewell. The rest is computer speak. 'swipe/your/card,' 'some/thing's/gone/down,' 'wa'any/fast/cash?'

Here she is again.

'Gingernuts? Round Wine? Chocolate Wheaten? Yes! Dougie likes those.'

I hurry to the cheese cooler and search for my favourite brie. She follows, parks her trundler in front and stretches across.

'Too dear! But lunches! Must have. Ah! Yogurt. I like a yogurt. Peach. Instore special!'

Glances. Why look at me? Me? It should be her.

I can't stand it. Don't want to know. Don't care.

Two melon breasts jamb me against the freezer. Words pump on to my skin, stick to my hair, dance around my earrings.

'Shampoo. Dog roll. Mustn't forget. Lemonade. Coupon. I've got one for that.'

'Excuse me,' I say loudly – well, I think it's loudly. Maybe it's only a thought. How would I know? 'Would you mind . . . ?' And I rattle my trolley.

She stares. And I know I don't exist. That her thoughts are words and my words are only thoughts. 'Pizza,' she says. 'Sunday pizza. Karen likes that. No peppers.' We're face to face, hip to hip. I look into her eyes and beyond see a trickling sand-picture forming and reforming. An overload of patterns changing before they can be fully comprehended.

And I know I must escape.

I run.

And as I run I hear screaming and see a figure racing past the frozen peas and chicken thighs, crashing through the checkout, ramming the smocked packer and disappearing through the self-opening glass doors.

Eyes. Eyes are startled. Shocked. But no one sees.

'Toothpaste, soap powder, vanilla.' The words echo. Follow. Engulf. 'Golden syrup, syrup, syrup . . .'

The doctor says I need a rest. Some therapy perhaps, but mostly a rest.

# Double Vision
## TONI QUINLAN

HE WAS IN the shower when the phone rang. Gemma, he thought. Little fool. Let it ring. She'd learn. He smoothed bath oil on chest and limbs, flexed muscles, admired the flat belly and even tan, stuck fingers in his ears, turned the mixer to invigorating cold. He stepped out on to the carpet, unhurriedly selected a hot towel from the rack.

The phone shrilled on. He smiled. She was a sweet kid, Gemma, a bit young perhaps, had taken it badly. She'd got serious. No need for that these days. He'd seen too many of his friends go that way. Look at them now. Half of them tied to kids and mortgages in the suburbs, the other half poor as mice after the split.

The ringing cut off. He peered into the mirror, grinned, stuck out his tongue, inspected his teeth. Francine, he thought, turning this way and that, Francine knew her way around. No problems there. No shortage of cash either, nice townhouse, smart little car. He allowed himself an anticipatory smirk. It should be a good evening.

When the phone rang again he picked it up quickly, his thoughts still on Francine. But it was Gemma. She must see him. It was urgent. Just for a few minutes. Please. A few seconds even. Tonight, now. Please . . .

He was firm, hiding his irritation with difficulty. Gem, my dear, it's over. You must accept that. In any case, I am going out tonight. Very soon.

She began to cry.

He put the receiver down gently, went to the sideboard, poured a generous whisky. That's the problem with young girls, he thought, frowning. It wouldn't have worked out. She hadn't a bean to her name. Extravagant too. The silver hipflask she had given him for his birthday must have put a dent in a week's pay and it wasn't even sterling. Plate. Cheap stuff. There was nothing in the pipeline either. Her people were small farmers, achingly ordinary folks, he could hear his friend Allister say. And dour with it, the old man especially. He hoped she wasn't going to cling. They usually got the message in the end.

He switched on the lights, adjusted the dimmers, chose a few unobtrusive CDs for later. Pacing, he replenished his glass, peered in the mirror over the mantel, fiddled with his tie, looked at his watch. Francine, Francine, come on, come on, let's get out of here. But his mind kept drifting back to Gemma, her freshness, her unpretentiousness, the way she deferred to him. Her hair, the aura of outdoors that always seemed to surround her.

Even though he was expecting it, the sound of the door knocker startled him. Francine! He snatched up his coat and keys, stowed away his wallet, smiled hello, flung open the door. But it was not Francine, it was Gemma.

He had time to see that she was still crying. Then she shot him, neatly and cleanly, between the eyes.

# Deprivation
## VALERIE MATUKU

THE AIR UNDER the blankets was hot and well used, having passed through her respiratory system several times. Morgan tossed aside the coverings, exhaled until her chest touched her spine, and then filled her lungs with cold bedroom air.

The rebreathing theory wasn't working. She had stayed under the blankets for fifteen minutes diligently using up the oxygen supply so that her brain would feel deprived. Linda had assured her that this was the stage when she would start having fantasies that could be turned into really weird stories. They were the ones that sold. The local library was stuffed full of fantasy and science fiction, so someone had to be buying and reading it. Romantic novels had all but disappeared from the shelves.

Morgan panted lightly, enjoying the idea of all the stuffiness passing out of her lungs to be freshened by the pot plants. Not much of a story there. The only plant story she could think of was *The Day of the Triffids*. Science fiction, of course. It was insidious stuff.

So why was the romance disappearing? Perhaps there had been a directive from the new Head Librarian. Morgan visualised a woman with a fiercely tethered bun withering at her demands for less fantasy and more romance. An interesting plot possibility. More romance . . . real men . . .

In the morning there was nothing in the bedside notebook. Linda said she had written brilliant things while suffering from oxygen deprivation, but obviously Morgan hadn't tried hard enough. The only revelation had been that of her romance depletion. The new Head Librarian would be sorted out this morning. Morgan might be starved of writing ideas, but she refused to be starved of her favourite reading material as well.

At nine o'clock she stood waiting on the library steps eyeing the full return box on the other side of the glass doors. Science fiction no doubt. Fantasy, sword and sorcery. All the stuff that was sweeping old-fashioned romance off the shelves. By the time a librarian unlocked the doors, she was ready for a showdown of impressive proportions.

The idea disappeared as soon as she met the new Head Librarian. He was romance and fantasy rolled into one, a living inspiration for poetry and prose.

'Ah, your fantasy section,' she said. 'I wanted to discuss it with you . . .'

'That's marvellous,' he said. His smile warmed and enveloped her like hot blankets. She dimly understood that it was oxygen loss creating the wonderful fantasies that whirled in her head. 'Another fan. You're enjoying my selections, then?'

'Yes,' she said. 'I love them. I've come to ask for more.'

# Happy Jack
## DAVID SOMERSET

THEY SAY HAPPY Jack caused the big fire in Wellington in 1886. He was one of that multitude of drifting men who, as the saying goes, 'earned their money like horses and spent it like asses'.

At the end of the day Happy Jack could usually be seen drinking in the hotels on Lambton Quay. He never had a home and either slept under the rose bushes in Parliament Grounds or crept secretly into buildings late at night. It was well known that he always smoked his pipe before falling asleep.

'Happy Jack'll burn down the colony one day!' the Lambton Quay shopkeepers said grimly. They were very nearly right.

The blaze began in a butcher's shop and spread to Smart's Oyster Saloon and Nelson's fruit shop. Then it turned up a lane off Woodward Street and invaded a group of cottages. In those days, fires were an exciting public event. People rushed from their houses and shouted with excitement as they saw a figure climb on to the ledge of an upstairs window.

'Jump! Jump!' the crowd yelled. Three cheers rang out as the figure bravely prepared to leap. But then the crowd fell strangely silent as they recognised Happy Jack. Fists were raised in the air and angry curses rang out. The firemen lost interest and no welcoming blanket now stretched below.

Happy Jack seemed doomed as the flames roared around him.

Just then a figure wearing a Salvation Army uniform was seen loping over the rooftops. The figure reached the parapet of the building, leaned right over, caught Happy Jack by the scruff of the neck and hauled him to safety.

'When I saw the blessed uniform of the Salvation Army above me,' Happy Jack said later, 'I was converted in a moment!'

No longer did Happy Jack spend days in the pubs and nights brawling along Lambton Quay. Instead he was in regular attendance when the Band of Hope marched up Willis Street on Friday nights. He set up outside Parliament Grounds as a street trader selling kittens, puppies, pigeons and goldfish.

Some unkind people claimed Happy Jack took his wares from the back gardens around Wellington. But he could point to his clientele, members of Parliament, as proof of his honesty.

Even Sir Julius Vogel stopped one day when Happy Jack had a litter of puppies for sale. 'Buy a puppy, Your Honour?' he said genially. 'All supporters of the Liberal Party. Guaranteed to bite any Conservative on sight!'

'Why, you scoundrel!' exclaimed Sir Julius. 'Last week you were selling the same ones as Conservative puppies!'

'Indeed, sir, that is true,' replied Happy Jack. 'But that was a week ago, when they were blind. Now they've grown a bit and their eyes are opened to the truth.'

# *Personally Seeking*
## NORMAN BILBROUGH

THE FIRST ONE had a big laugh with white teeth. Blonde, with wholesome eyes. Donna. Malcolm hadn't liked the way she moved. Too exuberant. Too outdoors. Kiss her and it would be like kissing fresh air. No intimacy about Donna.

But at least she hadn't picked a place like this. Malcolm gave a shudder when he arrived at the door: a vast hall full of gulping hordes.

But when he went in he could understand her tactic.

He'd thought about meeting her in a café. A brunette, showing off her stylish arms over a flat white – Malcolm locking in like a heat-seeking missile.

But what if she'd been another Donna: knocking over her coffee in her eagerness?

No escape from that situation.

The woman was called Jane. Not plain, her ad had assured. Slim, intelligent, into movies, ready to take chances. Attractive to men . . .

But . . . 'What's your interests?' she'd asked on the phone. There was a twang under the husky voice. Malcolm bet she forgot to be husky when she cleaned her teeth.

His interests? Sex, and more sex . . . Getting depressed . . . Eating food he couldn't afford.

'They vary,' he'd said. 'Lively conversation. Movies. I read a lot.'
'Are you tall?'
'Tallish.' He was short.
'What colour eyes?'
'Hazel. Serious eyes.'

'You got a gut?'

He'd laughed, sucking in his stomach. Pissed off though. He wouldn't say – You got big tits, or are you flat-chested?

She dropped the huskiness. 'What if we don't like each other?'

'We move on,' he'd said.


He stuck on his shades and moved through the eaters, looking for a brunette in a red suit. A liar . . . wearing too much make-up to cover her spots.

He spotted her easily. She was eating a meat thing. That was disgusting. He lingered a little way off. Her legs barely reached the floor and her nose was too big.

Malcolm took off his shades and moved closer. She had sensitive hands though – a surprise. She looked up. He moved by hastily.

He approached from another angle. She had her bag on a chair – reserved for him . . . A tall man with a big income, big house, big dick . . .

There was a fleck of food on her mouth. Malcolm was revolted – then remembered his dream. He was entering a paddock. The gate shut fast behind him. Donna was waiting. Donna was a horse: big, with overwhelming teeth. She was galloping towards him . . .

Malcolm stopped at the table. 'Is this seat taken?'

He wasn't wearing the red tie he said he would – and she had a sulky mouth. Better than Donna's mouth.

She was about to speak, and Malcolm said hastily, 'You aren't Jane, are you?'

She looked at him full in the face. And Malcolm got a shock: she gave him a harsh and intelligent scrutiny. Something that went far deeper than he believed in a twangy girl in a cheap red suit would own.

She shook her head abruptly. 'I'm Debbie,' she said, and turned away.

# Dempsey
## P. A. ARMSTRONG

IN THE HALF-LIGHT of that room we spoke in whispers. It seemed only right. Around the walls family pictures. Those of popes and a saint or two. Not forgetting our lady and child. Mastic on board low relief. Dempsey's framed coloured enlargement set to the fire's left. Born between Cliff and James. That would have made him my age had he lived. Now he sat. A small brown pharaoh propped up in state. More life in a teddy's eyes than his. From there we roamed countrywide. Fought guerilla warfare in chou moellier field. Out-flynning Flynn in brave dare-do. Cease fire commence fire. Our gallant leaders cried. Not sure which meant what. Shortage of manpower decreed. That those of us who. Died that day. Clutching our sides as tommy-gun bullets thudded home. Counted to thirty. Then lived to fight again. Climbed a cabbage tree. Because it was there. Quite easy once you manage the stem. A lily so Mr Roche had said. The biggest in the world perhaps. Well I never really checked that out. Another teacher was to say. Old Roche said that and laughed. Just short of adding 'the silly old bugger'. Gilded youth within a lily. Oh hardly read scruffy ragamuffin. Then across rolling hills we jiggery hopped. Came to a rocky outcrop. A desert island in that sea of green. There were other reefs. Roughage thrust through that matting of english grass english weeds. Nothing like this. Buttresses battlements pillars towers pinnacles beams flat tops. Forged in fire from earth centre. A stonehenge in rhyolite. Above our head stuffed in a crevice. Their nest like jute sacking. Wild bees to annoy. Higher still out of reach of cattle. And all but the most adventurous sheep. From soil that somehow collected there. Grew

manuka and giant kanuka. Fuchsia bracken nameless groundcover
lancewood ferns. We worldly we lit fires. Tried new swearing there.
Or ways of swearing newer still. Smoked stolen cigarettes. Imitating
our father's no-nonsense cough. With rabbiter's adze dug hand and
footholds in clay between rock. For drama losing hold crash . . .
sliding as far as ten feet to the flat. But in that front room where . . .
A hunched mantel clock chick-chicked out the hours. Where
Dempsey in his finery sat wedged up in state. We spoke in no more
than whispers it seemed only right.

# The Christening
## GRAEME LAY

LATER THE BOY could remember little of the ceremony. Men in suits, women in hats and gloves, crowding around the birdbath at the front of the church. Mrs Thomson handing her baby to the minister, his white surplice, the ripple of water, the intoned words. *Christopher Peter Andrew Thomson* . . . Then he and his parents got into their Morris Minor and drove to the Thomsons' house for the celebration.

'Such a lovely house, Duncan and Dorothy's,' said his mother as the car drew up outside. '*Two-storeyed.* He's done so well, Duncan, since he went out on his own.' The boy noticed a muscle in his father's jaw tighten. His mother took out her powder pack and dabbed at her face.

He followed his parents up the wide front steps, through the hall and into the lounge. It was easily the biggest house he had ever been in. Thick floral carpet, heavy furniture, paintings of mountains and rivers. An ornate staircase led up from the lounge. A *two-storeyed* house.

Mrs Thomson hugged his mother and Mr Thomson shook hands with his father. Mrs Thomson was short and stout and wore a bright red suit. Her husband was tall and dark-faced, with oiled hair. Mr Thomson poured his father a beer and his mother a sherry. The boy watched his mother staring around thoughtfully at the furniture, the paintings, the staircase. Then, as other adults arrived, he drifted to the back. He didn't know the other children there, didn't want to.

As he was helping himself to some salted peanuts from a bowl,

Mrs Thomson brought the baby in, wrapped in a blue shawl. Mr Thomson cleared his throat loudly and the room went quiet.

The speech wasn't long. He said something about, asked for their blessings on little Christopher, asked them to charge their glasses. Then the boy noticed something strange. No one except Mrs Thomson was looking at the baby. Usually everyone stared at babies, but now everyone was just looking down into their drinks. They drank the toast and Mrs Thomson took the baby out.

After she came back the boy slipped out of the room. On the other side of the hall was an open door. He went in.

It was a big room with yellow wallpaper patterned with animals. Cardboard animals – dozens of them – dangled from the ceiling. Cats, dogs, bears, giraffes. In the centre of the room was a bassinet covered with a lacy valance. The boy went up to it, peered in.

The baby was awake, staring upwards. Its head was large, the fair hair fine. Its blue eyes were close together. Much too close together. As the boy watched, the baby's eyes began to roll about. But what he thought strangest was the baby's tongue. It was too big for its mouth. It hung right out, shiny and pink, like a lamb's tongue from a tin.

The boy stared at the piggy face, the too-close eyes, the hanging tongue, for some time. Then he went out of the baby's room, to look for more food.

# *Jury Duty*
## ANITA SECCOMBE

I RODE THE escalator and nervously stepped off, following the arrows to the jury room. Inside, people were sitting, some reading the paper, others staring straight ahead. The only acknowledgement for new arrivals was a nod of some stranger's head. We sat. The silence of the room was deafening. One lady took out her knitting, looked around at the obviously idle-handed and started up a furious clicking with her plain and purl. It made the others feel edgy, irritated.

A clerk arrived and called names from precisely cut cards. Into the box they went to be shuffled. Those who were not called sighed with relief as they left the room in haste, smiling.

The rest of us sat, fear of the unexpected very real. We were led off into the courtroom, once more to repeat the process of names being pulled from the hat. Oh no, mine. Yes, I was present. The man before me had been challenged. He looked ordinary enough. The walk to the jury seat seemed interminable. No challenge. Oh gosh, what could the case be?

The two lawyers eyed the jurors up and down as their names were called. A young man in jeans, T-shirt and jerkin with long curly hair; a thirtyish man in a three-piece suit, neatly cut, smelling of aftershave; a woman, frizzy permed hair, long jersey over black tights. I tried to see if there was a pattern to the lawyers' choices. A middle-aged man who looked the typical father of three, then there was the painter, dressed in his overalls, cap and sandshoes. Challenge! The relief on his face was amusing; he was obviously only too keen to get back to his ceilings and walls. Finally, twelve citizens sat, staring straight ahead. Frozen.

The judge explained court procedure and we all found ourselves gliding into a system we were not only unfamiliar with, but with a language which, while used every day by the courts, was foreign to our ears.

The door opened. There stood the accused. Long black curly hair had not been brushed for the occasion. Black shirt and pants, neither washed nor ironed, dirty black boots. His shoulders were hunched and he swung his arms menacingly as he walked to the dock. From under hooded shaggy eyebrows he lifted his eyes. Slowly making eye contact with each juror. He stared them out, one, two, three . . . until finally the twelfth juror dropped her eyes.

The registrar read out his Christian names, surname, then the charge. *You are charged with assaulting and causing grievous bodily harm on a day and time of the previous year. How do you plead?*

He once again glared at the jury, then, slowly lifting his chin, sneered towards the judge.

The jury froze, in anticipation of his response.

# The Day . . .
## SUE McCAULEY

. . . they arrested him I was mending our deck chair.

I'd been planning to repair it for several months. The canvas had rotted and to replace it I had knitted an oblong of shiny blue synthetic fibre I had bought many years before at a fire sale. It was the fibre's second incarnation. Its previous existence had been as a shirt for my husband. He only wore it twice. It looked like baby-blue chain armour and he wasn't the crusading kind. When he went he left the shirt behind and I'd kept it in case; unravelling a sleeve a year, waiting for a deck chair to come into my life.

I was attaching one end of this shiny blue creation to the bottom of the chair with a piece of old blind rail to keep it firm when his wife arrived. She was in tears. She said they'd come and taken him away without a word to her. She was upstairs and she'd looked out the window and seen her husband walking away between two policemen. They had walked in just like repo men and removed her husband.

I didn't know what to say or do, so I kept on fixing the deck chair. I tried to imagine how it would feel to look out the window and see your husband walking away between two policemen, but nothing came.

It seemed to me very important that I should finish fixing the chair. I had the feeling that repairing the chair was a thread that could lead to the meaning of the universe. She sat at a table and cried while I hammered in three nails and five tacks. It took quite a long time because I am unskilled at carpentry.

When it was finished my son wanted to try out the chair. He

needs to be first to do everything, which is a cross his sister has to bear. He sat down in the chair with confidence and the plastic knitting stretched until he hit the floor. We laughed at the look on his face. Her husband had been taken away and put in a cell, but the woman laughed at this kid lying in the deck chair with his bum flat on the floor.

She wiped her face, then asked if she could use the phone to ring her friend in the city. I was feeling disappointed about the chair and all my efforts for nothing. I edged the claw of the hammer beneath the blind rail to prise it loose. And I listened to her using the phone. *Hey*, she said first thing to her friend, *you'll never guess. After I left you last Friday I went back and bought that ridiculous dress.*

*I just couldn't resist it.*

# Broken China
## RICHARD BROOKE

MR FREEMAN WAS old but remained a curious man. He had recently travelled to China to discover, on a personal level of course, the fallout from that decade known in the West as the Great Cultural Revolution. He had weighed up the word 'fallout' back home in Pontypool, read a lot of books, but had always felt he would be better to come here, to reach out in this ancient country and touch the truth for himself. The Pontypool Library, it had to be said, was a dark and unfriendly place at the best of times.

He had walked through the dusty magic of Beijing at dusk, marvelling at the way the swallows soared on the wind gusts. The bicycle bells trilled in his head as he blew his nose. This morning he had touched the hem of the curtain in his hotel room and received an electric shock. It was so unexpected that he knew coming here was exactly the right thing to do. But also, something marvellous. Yesterday he had met Wang, a statistician, who invited him to tea.

Wang told him he was a survivor of Mao's great experiment, and now, after all these years, Mr Freeman felt a little light-headed as he climbed the stairs to Wang's apartment in one of the austere Beijing towers. He knocked at the door and waited. The corridor smelled of boiled cabbage and the air was thick with coaldust.

'Come in.'

Wang's voice was soft and inviting, reminding Mr Freeman of the small Qing dynasty gong he had on his desk at home. He called it the Whisper Gong.

'Come around to my home,' Mr Wang had said. 'We'll eat together.'

Wang worked all day with numbers in a government office. Lunar numbers, Mr Freeman muttered to himself later in his hotel room and, if pressed, he would have conceded that all those zeroes left him exhausted.

They ate dumplings and looked out the window at the snow which was now falling.

'I can't really tell you anything.' Wang shrugged. 'China is so many things.'

Mr Freeman's attention was drawn to the curtain stretched across the room. He knew that Wang's wife was living in another city, but he had the distinct feeling someone was behind the curtain. Naturally he was too polite to ask. There was a burst of coughing, which Wang ignored.

'Sometimes I feel angry . . .' Wang's voice drifted off and he spread his hands out in a gesture that might have been acceptance. Mr Freeman couldn't be sure. There was a cry from behind the curtain. Mr Freeman, startled, dropped his cup on the floor. It shattered on the hard concrete and the white fragments lay like so many sad bones.

'I'm sorry.'

'It's nothing.'

Mr Freeman bent down to pick up the pieces.

'Forget it,' Wang said, and stood up, going over behind the curtain. Mr Freeman sat and waited.

'Pull back the curtain please,' Wang called out.

The Chinese statistician was sitting on a raised bed beside an old woman whose white hair was tied in a long pigtail. She lay back on the green and gold quilt, wearing a long, dull grey gown. Wang was holding one of her feet in his hand. The tiny, misshapen thing rested in his palm. He was massaging it. 'It is sometimes painful for her, you know. She is old. She can remember the Emperor,' Wang said.

The old woman stared at Mr Freeman. He dropped his eyes in confusion. She said something to Wang. 'What did she say?' Mr Freeman asked.

Wang smiled. 'She said she was glad I had a foreign friend. Maybe you will help me go to America.'

'Tell her I'm Welsh,' Mr Freeman said.

Wang whispered something in the old woman's ear, and she laughed. A dry, empty sound. Mr Freeman was looking around for a brush to remove the broken cup.

'She says it is the same thing.'

# Ash
## VIRGINIA WERE

SHE STANDS IN the scorched paddock, holding the metal box with her name taped to the outside, McKinnon – to be collected. *What should I do?* she asks. The box is heavy and she remembers the sharp pain when he stood on her foot, the way he would lean his head on her shoulder so that she felt the clean, curved edge of his jaw. She remembers lessons during the wetter season when the ground held his imprint – crescent moons in the grass on days when it rained.

At night when the wind died down and everything grew quiet she could hear him outside the bedroom window, a steady, rhythmic chewing. Sometimes, unable to sleep, she stood on the dewy lawn as stars wheeled and fell and the world tilted towards morning. His big white shape helped it along, shoving the darkness aside to make way for the grainy, uncertain dawn.

She tears the tape and lifts the lid. *Here?* she asks, not wanting to be seen. *No, over by the trees.* She scoops a handful of coarse coral and, turning her back on the road, the horses and riders, the white paling fence, begins to scatter what the heat has left. Her arm describes an arc, throwing grain to invisible hens or sowing seeds at the base of trees.

She is absorbed in this movement, the sound of him like rain in the grass. She rubs him between her fingers. Pink and apricot, as white as a beach. As if in deference to the occasion it begins to rain, the first rain in the worst drought in living memory. *The park is quiet for a Saturday,* she says as she returns him to the ground.

# Sibyl's Psychic Hotline
## JON THOMAS

THE LAST DAY of May, a Friday, at lunchtime, Bella threw a Cream of Chicken Cup-a-Soup that smashed against the wall beside Con's head. Con shut herself in the kitchen, wedged the door, sobbed.

Bella's face had a shine to it, waxy, like the skin of a drum. The way she curled herself up in the bed, she seemed to have shrunk away to nothing. She had been such a burly, lusty woman; in a helpless, hapless way her big brown eyes were as beautiful to Con as ever, but Con didn't know what else she could do.

She wouldn't eat. Con prepared her favourite meals, but Bella shoved the food around and pushed the tray away. She would only drink water, and only then when she moved from the bed to use the bathroom and could draw it from the tap herself. They hadn't made love since April.

'You could have cholera and I'd still want to cuddle into you,' Con whispered through the door.

'It's all your bloody fault!' screamed Bella.

Strangely, it wasn't something Bella had ever believed in. When Con read out their horoscopes, Bella always said, 'Don't you see? That crap fits in with everything.' Con said, 'Our biographies are signed and sealed from the moment of conception.' 'Bollocks,' said Bella.

Con spent all her money trying to discover tomorrow. 'Bloody waste,' said Bella, who spent her own on tattoos, mostly a blend of daggers and barbed wire. 'I'll shout you for your birthday though,' Con said, and persuaded Bella to telephone the Psychic Hotline:

$2.99 per minute – Sibyl's Vision of the Future. Con listened in on the bedroom extension.

What Sibyl described was Bella's father doing things to Bella that only Bella knew about. Con's mouth fell open; Bella's face turned the colour of bone.

During the silence that followed, Con imagined Sibyl's jewelled fingers arranging the cards on a green-baize table.

They heard a sudden intake of breath.

'We're paying you for this,' Bella said at last.

When Sibyl spoke again, there was a thread of panic in her voice. 'It's a blank,' she said. 'I can't see you beyond the end of May.'

Then a click. The telephone went dead.

For four weeks they lived in a state of anguished irony.

Come midnight, and Saturday the first of June, Bella, with her eyes shut tight, was concealed beneath their eiderdown.

From the kitchen Con called out, 'It's time.'

Bella leaps from the bed, grabs the telephone, dials the number, yells, 'I'm going to have a piece of you, Madam bloody Sibyl!' but finds instead another voice, a man's, a recorded message, murmuring regret, thanking her for responding to his recent loss.

# The Bach
## PATRICIA DONNELLY

THE OLD COTTAGE sat in a heap on the beach, just by the landward end of the wharf. It looked as if it was waiting for the next boat out – had been waiting for such a long time that it had given up hope.

The island had passed through a variety of hands since last century, when its Maori owners had, by all accounts, been judicially robbed. No doubt it was due to feature in some future land claim, but that would be somebody else's worry.

My job was to see that everything was ready for the developers to move in. That would mean bulldozers, barged across the narrow strait on a calm day. The two or three modern holiday homes, mostly on the far side of the island, could stay. They'd have company soon, and lots of it, with time-share apartments, a caravan camp and, it was hoped, a casino. Pleasure Island, the brochures were calling it.

The wharf was sound enough, and there was a metalled track that ran inland, past the dilapidated building. I paused at the sagging door with its rusty horseshoe – all the luck run out of it. The old man had told me, last night in the pub on the mainland, that the bach had been used as a builders' hut from time to time. The gangs would stay there, weeks on end, augmenting their diet of tinned food with fresh oysters from the rocks.

Nobody lives there now, he said. But there used to be an old girl – not that I ever saw her myself. Went across when the ferry was still running and missed the last one back, so they say.

Even with the door left open, the interior was dark. Shadowy furniture – of sorts – still waited for the next occupant. Like the building itself, it was made from odds and ends – timber, driftwood, corrugated iron. Things the builders hadn't needed, even salvage from the occasional shipwreck from the look of it. All held together with cobwebs and dust. We wouldn't need the bulldozer, I thought – one man with a sledgehammer could bring the whole lot down.

Just the one room. A heap of rags on a sagging bedframe in one corner served as sleeping quarters. No electricity. A nearby stream supplied all the usual conveniences.

Blackened frypan, empty beer bottles, and on the shelf beside them, a handful of paperback books. Romances, most of them. The story about the old girl squatting here must be true, then. I wondered where she'd gone.

A spiral-bound notebook caught my eye. Picking it up, I tried to decipher the pencil scrawl. Now and again the odd word would stand out, making me feel curiously uneasy.

Then, returning to the first page, I read: *The old cottage sat in a heap on the beach, just by the landward end of the wharf. It looked as if it was waiting for the next boat out.*

# Cocktail Conversation
## DIANE BROWN

THIS LAWYER AT the bar, plying me with Tequila Sunrises, could become my lover. He is wearing a heavy gold bracelet. I pretend I am a woman of potential, weaving urban myths and personal history into matted anecdotes. My friend, Jill, has left. Her husband requires her to be home by midnight. There is no one waiting for me. 'Do you believe in arranged marriages?' I ask.

I tell him the wedding should have been perfect. The bride and groom beautifully matched. Perhaps it was the memory of the steak eaten at the stag do, perhaps it was the lack of breakfast, but whatever the reason the groom couldn't wait. Taking one look at his bride, he sank his teeth into her breast. The blood dripped over the bouquet of yellow roses, but the guests carried on eating. They were Siberian tigers, but even so.

The rose outside my conservatory is pale pink and has no relation to this conversation at all, except that I think of roses as I nod my head in a parody of consciousness. Waiting for him to cut me with innocent questions. 'What's wrong with you? Why did your husband leave you?' I am wet with dew and slippery enough.

'I needed a change of colour in the garden. I gave him a list of airline departures and went back to pruning the roses. Do you know you must cut on an angle, above an outward-gazing eye?'

Rupert is wondering why I am giving him tips on gardening. Clearly he doesn't know my mother. But he is not thinking about me. He wants to talk about Jill. She is his type, slinky and quiet. 'Why aren't you like her?' he asks. 'She knows a good thing or two. How to hang on to her man. He's one of the best, you know.' And I don't, having only heard her side of the marriage, seen the invisible trails of abuse left on the surface of her mind.

'Western women talk too much,' Rupert says. He has been to Japan. Geishas are taught how to listen. Words pushed into every orifice. Make-up caked on so thick, clients can relax, knowing the real person's face is deep beneath and impenetrable. Only the mouth opening enough to permit a small, agreeable smile.

Rupert is curious to know the fate of the tigers. He tells me he was once tricked into marriage. Perhaps the arranged may be better. 'At least you get someone from the same background with the same attitudes.'

He orders a Virgin Caesar for himself and asks if I want a Screaming Orgasm. I reply, 'No. I'm going home now to my roses.' I am anxious to leave before I give too much away. Before I tell him the bride got up to dance, despite the blood. Before his bracelet catches on my lace blouse.

# *Skin Room Female*
## ELIZABETH SMYTH

AT FIRST YOU think you'll spend the money on a trip to Spain. Then you go to the opening of this exhibition. There's all the usual there . . . suits and wallys and the black-uniform crowd, all sashaying around big dripping canvasses, holding their wine glasses in front of them like annoying afterthoughts.

The crowd dwindles. You see a smaller work tucked in the corner. Suddenly it's like those films you've seen where there's two people in a room with eyes only for each other. Except that this time it's you and a painting singing a song together, like whales tracking each other out at sea.

It's not often that paint and colour and essence hit you, haunt you like this. When you were little, your parents had a big book called *National Art Treasures*. You used to open it and gaze at a painting by Picasso. You ingested all its colours and knew the exact expression on the clown's face. At the dinner table you would pretend you were the clown, leaning on your elbows, looking into a glass, until someone nudged you and you had to pass them something.

. . . A woman with a bird's head stands on top of a large Victorian table covered with a white cloth, dressed in Victorian grey. As if on stage she stands erect, the Pacific Ocean her backdrop. Pongas drip with the denseness of thick moisture. She looks out to her left, away from an object she is holding, a harp, or maybe a bird skin, you're not sure. Perhaps she is singing a lament. She is the 'Skin Room Female'.

'It's all about *Buller's Birds*,' says your friend. 'You know, the Victorian artist? Well, this painter talks about what he was really up to. Not many people know the bugger caused our birds to become extinct. She's a huia. Buller drew them and at the same time was knocking them off for their skins, until well, you know the rest.'

That night, instead of dreaming about Spain and the castanets, you find yourself in an old world of bush and waterfalls. Birds sing and dart about among the green leaves that hang heavy with rain. Suddenly there is a bang and you awaken.

The framer said a black background would be best. Your partner said he didn't mind if you bought it, he wasn't all that into Spain. You hoped he was telling the truth, because two months later he moved out. Perhaps it was because of the painting. With the frame and the matt, it was pretty large and so, to make it fit, you took down his poster of the flamenco dancer and pinned it in the spare room.

Spring came. You found a cheaper place to stay. It wasn't that big, but you didn't have much stuff. Just you, some junk and the painting. Waiting for the uninterrupted song.

# *Salvation*
# LOUISE WRIGHTSON

IN THE LAST twenty minutes before the world ended, the phone lines jammed (as you'd expect). Max McLean, in the South Island for a conference, couldn't get through to his dear wife Kate to confess to a two-year affair with her best friend. His dear wife Kate couldn't get through to her best friend to confess she hadn't loved Max for the last two years.

Sylvia, the best friend, was in bed with their butcher, who kept moaning – breasts ribs shins shanks flanks, and some other cuts Sylvia hadn't heard of. She wished there was enough time to explain that that sort of chat didn't do anything for her. It only confirmed a suspicion that vegetarians had something to offer after all, at this late stage.

Instead, she closed her eyes, rolled over on her belly (RUMP! roared the butcher) and thought about her roses until he left, ruddy and sated, promising fillet the next night. He can't have been in the know. Not everyone was.

In the last ten minutes before the world ended, Sylvia threw back the sheets and ran into the garden. The evening smelt yeasty, like warm, fresh bread. The buttercups and daisies had closed forever (amen). Cats flickered in the bushes, hunting their last blackbird bye-bye. Sylvia thought of climbing to the top of the walnut tree and singing 'Auld Lang Syne' as a final extravagant gesture, but decided against it. Life was too short.

In the last few minutes before the world ended, Sylvia knelt, not to pray, but to weed around her roses. Puffs of dark perfume mixed with the sharp smell of mulch, and a last bright shaft of sunlight lay across her plump back.

In the last ten seconds before the world ended, a hot orange wind zapped out of the evening sky. It turned the pine trees into giant candles, curled the garden vines like pubic hair, incinerated the butcher as he hummed happily home and whipped a rose branch around Sylvia's wild red head of hair.

So our Sylvia, sinner, was first through the gates of Heaven – naked, hands covered in cowshit, wearing a crown of thorns.

# *Jinx*
# TINA SHAW

SHE STOOD ON the Bridge of Remembrance and threw chopped rhubarb leaves into the water, whispering a mantra. 'You are going to have an accident, you are going to get hurt, your four-wheel-drive yuppie car is going to collide with a very large truck . . .' She had eyes that were ringed with black eyeliner and wore a waistcoat over a short top with the maxim 'Golf is for Suckers' across her breasts.

What happened was that she had done some artwork and then they didn't use it and tried not to pay her by saying that it was crap, but she must be paid and Tucker was insisting that she take them to the Small Claims Court, the bastards, and Tucker should know, he had taken several people through the Small Claims Court. 'He fancied me, of course,' she told Tucker, who nodded wisely.

And then what made matters worse was that the Rat had sent her a crushed chrysalis in a box. It was black, the tiny golden dots still visible. She had retched at the foot of the letterbox. She had the box clutched now in her hand: an evil amulet to fuel a jinx.

She walked off the bridge, confident that something horrible was going to happen to the Rat because she had set it off, she had laid the jinx. It would work, it was just a matter of believing.

Pedro was driving across the bridge, unaware of rhubarb leaves floating below. He hadn't meant for the artwork to become such a problem. After all, she was always late, and it was crap – what were you supposed to do? They had had to get someone else to do the whole job again. It had cost more money. He hadn't meant to tell her that her boyfriend was a useless son-of-a-bitch and that all she wanted was a father figure. And he had even sent her a gift, thinking to patch up ill feelings: a butterfly chrysalis in a box. It would hatch, said the card, into a beautiful monarch butterfly.

He noticed at the last moment that a large truck was looming across his path. A Mack, filling the windscreen. He swerved madly, steering wheel spinning. Fortunately the other lane was empty. 'Oh shit,' he breathed.

'You are going to have an accident, you are going to get hurt . . .' She was walking past the River Café when she spotted Tucker outside. She started over to tell him about the jinx. Then she noticed that he was sitting with a woman who had straight blonde hair that was so long it lay in her lap. Where Tucker's hand was resting like an earwig.

She screamed. And hurled the chrysalis box at Tucker, wheeling away. The chrysalis, freed from its box, landed in the foam of Tucker's cappuccino, where it sank as gracefully as a newborn jinx.

# *Window Dressing*
## THOMAS MITCHELL

IT WAS THE second time that he'd thrown up. Leo was nervous.

— What's it to be, Leonard? Robert said.

Leo struggled up from the railing and walked back to the car.

— I'm going in. I can't ask again.

Robert smiled. Then I'll drop you off, he said.

It was fifteen minutes into town from Devonport. Robert sat at the lights while Leo got his jacket and a handful of mints from the glovebox.

— Shall I pick you up?

— Nah, I'll make my own way home. Never know, might get lucky, Leo said.

They sniggered and Robert drove off in the old car, smoking and growling at the congestion.

It looked like a good night. Groups of people were on Queen Street, laughing and talking. A restaurant had put out tables on a balcony. It was bustling. But there were too many out-of-towners and window-shoppers standing around watching buskers and street preachers. He had to fight to get through. People walked together like nets drifting down the street, so when he got to the bar he was late.

Alex sat waiting, looking up as Leo came in. Those impenetrable eyes.

— Are you always this late?

Leo grimaced and shrugged.

— I've already bought the tickets, Alex said.

Leo was surprised. He had imagined that they would choose the movie together after talking. Something European with subtitles.

— Yeah, which flick? he said.

— The new Van Damme movie. I hope you like it.

— Great, I saw the reviews, he said.

The reviews were rubbish. It had only raised a single digit from Siskel and Ebert. European with submachine guns. He hoped the choice hadn't been for his sake.

They got seats near the back. A bald man came in and sat down in front of them. The projector lights caught the back of his head. Leo watched as gun fights and fist fights glimmered on the pate. Dark sand storms on the surface of Mars.

Alex put a hand on Leo's leg. He froze. It wasn't what he expected from a first date. A kiss, perhaps, at the door, but a hand on his leg was something else. He could feel Alex's fingers burning a hole through his thigh. His stomach churned inward.

When it was over, they went out into the foyer. Alex was smiling. An enjoyable movie. Eyes sparkling in the light. Expectation. More to come. Leo excused himself to go to the bathroom. He felt like being sick again, but instead found himself pushed out a side entrance with all the other patrons coming out. The door closed behind them and he was locked out. The entrance was around the corner. There were lots of shop windows closer, on the other side. He could see his reflection and began to walk along looking into them. He could pick out the dress he liked most before he got to the ferry.

# Chain of Events
## PATRICIA GRACE

MARIA HUNG HER jacket behind the door and put on her smock, ready to dish up. Mrs Jackson came in and told her that there'd been some cutting back and that from now on clients would not be allowed second helpings.

The door opened and the first lot came in, shuffling, stumbling, clenching teeth, flapping an arm, dragging a leg, making noises. The ones who were able lined up with their plates, while the client-aids sat the others down at the tables to have their meals brought to them.

Maria began serving out and it wasn't a bad day because all the clients arrived at the tables without accidents, sat down and began chomping the food, which was lukewarm so they wouldn't burn themselves. They used plastic spoons with which they could do no harm, shovelling and swallowing.

While they were eating the mince and vegetables Maria dished out the puddings and put them ready on the counter. She pushed the trolley out front so that clients and helpers could scrape and stack their first lot of dishes and put their cutlery in the basin of soapy water. After that they could get the puddings, which they would eat quickly so they could come up for seconds.

Darlene with the rashes, who was always first, stood up, splitting her dress under both armpits, jolting the table and making the dishes jump while her chair went sliding. She came stamping up to the counter, looking pleased, calling, 'Maria, Maria.'

Maria had to tell Darlene that Mrs Jackson had said that she wasn't allowed to give anyone seconds now, that there wasn't any more because it was all dished up the first time. She had to show Darlene the empty dish and tell her over and over until she understood.

Then Darlene threw her bowl, punched her fist through a window and fell down with a wide spike of glass through her wrist. When one of the client-aids pulled the piece of glass out, blood began spurting everywhere and there was loud noise with plates and chairs falling and people shouting.

The ambulance came and Darlene was taken to hospital while the other clients, laughing and crying, were taken away so that the cleaning up could be done. Security was sent for and a few old boards were nailed up over the window.

That night Maria had nightmares in which she was spooning up bloody tapioca while Darlene stood by her laughing and laughing, both arms severed.

When she went to work the next day and asked about Darlene, Mrs Jackson said, 'Still in hospital, good job, serve the silly bitch right, always throwing her weight around upsetting the place. Pity she didn't put her head through.'

Maria hung her jacket behind the door and put on her smock, ready to serve the food as the first ones came through the door.

# The Marquesas Maybe
## GRAEME LAY

'I DECIDED THAT before I die I'd see the world. So last year I chucked it all in – marriage, house, job – and bought myself a yacht. Do it, mate, while you've still got your health, I told myself. After all, you're a long time lookin' at the lid.'

He reached for a cigarette from the packet on the table between us. His arms were thin and stringy, the skin burned dark by the tropical sun. His hands shook as he lit the cigarette. We were sitting in the bar of a cheap hotel on the Apia waterfront. Minutes earlier we had been at separate tables. Then the old man had beckoned me over, bought me a beer.

'Are you married?' he asked.

'Not yet.'

He nodded. 'Everyone has to try it, I suppose. But in the end you have to get out. Kills a man's spirit.'

His face was fleshless, the bones of his cheeks and forehead visible under the dark, shrivelled skin. He had no upper front teeth and the lower ones were just grey, bevelled stumps. His faded blue T-shirt hung in folds around his upper arms.

'How long have you been at sea?' I asked.

'Four months. I bought *Liberty* last January, from a Yank. I lived in a caravan in Opua after the divorce came through, waited for the right boat to come on the market. Took navigation classes while I waited. Then one day she came along. *Liberty.* Even her name was right. Month later I was at sea.'

'Where are you going next?'

'Pago. After that, Rangiroa. The Marquesas maybe.' He looked over to the harbour. 'Liberty's moored out there, in front of Aggie's.'

'Any problems, sailing solo?' *At your age*, was the unspoken adjunct to my question.

He chuckled. 'One or two. Nearly hit Minerva Reef. Got through on me third try. Stayed there a week, living off lobsters and beer.'

He picked up his Vailima, drank. His Adam's apple bobbled inside his thin, crêpey neck. Good on you, I thought. How many old people just sat around in some geriatric holding pen, minds and bodies crumbling, with nothing to look forward to except death? But this old bloke was going to go out with his spinnaker flying.

'People said I was mad. They knew I'd smoked and drunk too much all me life. They thought I'd never make it out of the Bay of Islands. But I showed them.' He cackled. 'Just getting rid of that bloody woman gave me another ten years, I reckon.'

He put his glass down, looked into the distance, past the sea wall, towards where the little flotilla of yachts bucked against the trade wind. His grey hair was sparse on top, long and curling at the ends. Knowing how the elderly wear their age like a medal, I said, 'How old are you now?'

He turned back to me, cocked his head proudly. 'Next birthday,' he said, 'in a fortnight's time, I'll be fifty-six years of age.'

# The Seventies
## JANE WESTAWAY

A MAN I knew slightly suggested we go outside and take off my bra. Hippies, he said with authority, did not wear bras.

The invitation had said a barn dance. That meant hay bales, a plodding band manned by farmers' sons, and greenery festooning the walls of someone's woolshed. It had also said come as a hippie, but we had only the remotest idea of what this might entail. We opted for ragbag clothes, the odd joke wig and a lot of guffawing about pot and free love – both as yet unavailable in this part of the world.

Alone behind the woolshed, the man and I became decorous. I said, excuse me; he turned his back. Still, we returned breathless with daring. My husband asked what I had been doing, knitting his eyebrows and setting his mouth in the line that four years of marriage had taught me to dread. He'd made no effort on the hippie front – except for the clowns, men were not expected to. If you'd asked any of those lumbering through the Gay Gordons that night, they would have jovially avowed the country creed: it's what's underneath that counts, especially out here. Fads mean nothing. The real things don't change.

And I would have agreed, standing there in clothes I thought appropriate for making love not war, listening to my husband in his tweed jacket talk of wool prices and pasture growth. Yet there was something about the feel of flowing purple, the T-shirt soft against my breasts, the swinging beads, the hay-strewn floor underfoot. Something that, when the man who'd helped remove my bra said he was off on someone's bike to pick up more beer, made me say gaily, I'll come.

I was shocked by the speed, the terrifying angle when we cornered, how I had to cling to the man's broad back. The ride left me breathless, light-headed, which I could claim made it impossible to resist when he led me through the house and lay me and the flowing purple across his bed. Except that it might have been me who led him.

I heard later his wife was furious about the slick of motorbike grease on her aqua candlewick bedspread. And when the man and I returned to the woolshed, my husband refused to speak except to demand we leave immediately.

The man and I had not done everything – or even most things – on the aqua candlewick. I remained a good wife and mother under the silly clothes, of course I did, and the next day I buttoned my sensible blouse, returned the long beads to my daughter's dress-up trunk and apologised to my husband. He accepted graciously enough, but until the day in 1975 when I packed the kids into the station wagon and drove out of the farm for the last time, I would catch him looking at me as if he were no longer fooled.

# The Things That Can't Be Named
## DIANNE TAYLOR

STELLA IS LEARNING to put names to things. She'd expected that university would reveal how much she didn't know. What she hadn't anticipated was that so many of her own half-formed, fleeting thoughts would be dignified and concretised with names and terms and theories. It was reassuring to know that she wasn't the only one who had wondered where God got the Ten Commandments from. Or why an elephant is called an elephant and not a bubble, or a bulldozer, or a megaloptus.

'Diphthongs', for example. Six weeks ago she might have suggested, only half jokingly, that they were jandals worn by nerds. Now she could write an essay about New Zealand vowel and diphthong sounds and get an A plus for it. The A plus was satisfying, but not half as satisfying as having an answer for James when he points out over dinner on the first night of their holiday that despite her grades she still pronounces 'milk', 'mulk'.

'It's the broad New Zealand centralised i,' she explains patiently. 'It turns "milk" into "mulk" and "fish and chips" into "fush and chups".'

'Well it sounds common,' says James.

'It is common,' says Stella. 'But not the way you mean it. It's a non-stigmatised indicator of the New Zealand dialect. It's the way New Zealanders speak.'

'It's not the way I speak,' James says, taking particular care to round his vowels. He lived in Britain for three years a decade ago and thinks he speaks BBC English. Stella explains to James that he's merely displaying linguistic insecurity and linguistic prejudice, which is just as bad as racial prejudice and is a sign of ignorance.

'At least I don't say "mulk",' says James. And Stella tells him that she's fucked if she's going to change the way she speaks for his ignorant benefit. She knows she's right. Which is all very well, except that now she's sitting, crying, in a too-many-patterned cheap hotel room in Napier with an air ticket back to Auckland in her hand, and James is halfway to Wellington to catch the night ferry to the South Island.

Two days ago, when they chose this room for its quirk-value, the mismatched curtains, wallpaper, carpet and bed coverings amused them. Two days ago she hadn't put a name to the thing she hated most about James. A four-letter word beginning with S. 'Snob.' A superior, self-deceiving, sycophantic snob. The spluttering stream of sibilants give her a measure of satisfaction. James wouldn't know sibilance if he was stuck in a cesspit full of serpents. She knows she's right. So why is she crying?

She's crying for the things that still don't have a name. The things she'll never understand. Like how the word 'love' can come to mean 'hate'. Or why the threads of their lives have woven a shroud for a dead relationship. She's crying for the things they don't teach at university.

# The Optician
## JUDITH WHITE

HE TOLD HER to look into his eye, so that he could adjust her new glasses. She always found it embarrassing to be forced to gaze into a stranger's eye, in such a cold mechanical way. Like sex without love. But she did as she was directed, expecting to see his iris, his brown murky iris with the petroleum-dark pupil, as she had witnessed on other occasions. But instead she saw the moon, a bright full moon with all its craters and mountains. She suspected it might be a trick, and then realised that he, too, was looking flustered and puzzled.

'Will you come out with me?' he said.

'All right then,' she muttered.

She prepared for the date with trepidation. What should she wear? He hadn't said where he would take her. She finally selected a short black dress with a long black shawl embroidered with golden swirling leaves. On the bed was a high pile of discarded clothes. She wondered whether he would come home for the night. She shoved the clothes under the bed.

As it happened, he arrived on the doorstep looking eager and nervous. He was dressed in jeans and a silken turquoise shirt. He said, 'I know a little café by the beach where we can have something to eat.'

'Okay,' she said.

He parked the car by the waterfront. 'Let's have a quick look at the sea,' he suggested.

'Terrific,' she replied.

Their shoes sank into the fresh dry sand. The sea made little whispery lappy noises, over and over. The sky was petroleum black like his eyes, and the moon dangled above them. They both looked at it, then turned to each other. Each of them had a sense of destiny, of having been hurtled towards this moment from the beginning of their existence. He wanted to kiss her, but felt she might misinterpret his intentions. She wanted to hold him forever, but felt he might think she was stupid and clinging. They both told themselves that there was plenty of time for all that.

Oh dear.

Little did they know. That was their moment, and they missed it.

'Oh well, let's have dinner,' he said warmly, and they headed towards the restaurant, an intimate shadowy place with candles on the table. She ordered a fish dish in a brown creamy sauce, and by the end of the evening felt quite ill. He was safe with a steak, but their conversation flagged alarmingly, and he realised he must have imagined everything.

By the time they walked back to the car, the moon was behind a cloud and she could think of nothing but that she hoped she made it home before she was sick.

Afterwards, when she didn't hear from him, she changed her optician. When she didn't return for her glasses, he was almost relieved. However, both of them, for a while, felt bewildered and confused.

# Go and Catch a Falling Star
## LAURIS EDMOND

DOES SHE REALLY have to do it, this costly uncomfortable thing? Really, your kids when they grow up turn into aliens, bossy strangers who constantly underestimate you. She herself is so mild, so accommodating – it's as though their roles are grotesquely reversed. Three months, they say. Well, she'll show them.

Trapped, even before they leave the ground, she feels the intense closeness of the next seat. A man, one who stares. Yet he's good-looking, grey, brushed. Sleek.

'Zees is nice, ees it not?' Well, well, a foreigner. She barely acknowledges him, spreads the hairy cotton blanket, turns away. She will say no to magazines, food, certainly to conversation. And eventually the hostess's ghastly patter does fade, the lights dim; meaningless jumble appears on the screen. A-ah –

At first it's the merest stirring, like an animal waking up; it becomes a movement. A hand. Fingers. Warm flesh. Can it be her own hands? They are in her lap after all. But no, these turn, stroke, insinuate. They begin to insist. Indeed they advance. Her face turns bright red in the dark. She feels her body loosen, slacken, ease its moistening orifices.

But then she stiffens. What kind of vulgar creature can she be, for God's sake? A mindless idiot? A kid without the least experience of the world? A solitary nobody . . . She straightens her back, stretches her ankles. Leaves the middle portions as they are, however, while she urgently considers her options.

1. Sit up, turn on the overhead light, whip off the blanket, say, There's room for fucking (could she say this?) at the end,

against the wall, outside the toilets. Not here.

2. Let him go on, see how inventive he is, respond as the whim dictates. Be a devil.

3. Poke him hard with the sharp end of a nail file, if she can reach it. Small neat gestures – her own hands are still free.

4. Take his hands and hold them, ask him to talk about his life, explaining she understands his needs.

5. Turn the light on and tell him how interesting her children are now they're growing up . . .

6. Call the hostess and have him removed.

Stealthily she feels along the arm rest for switches. As she tenses, her handbag, lurking on the far side of her lap, slithers fast and heavily across the blanket. The activity beneath stops at once, a kind of grunt erupts. Almost at the same moment the beam of a torch light flickers brutally across their faces.

'Excuse me, Señor Ambassador, extremely sorry to disturb you, but – we – have a problem on board. One of your countrymen . . . a case of mistaken identity, we believe . . . the captain has an urgent phone message – your office in Valparaiso. I would not think of disturbing you, señor, but under the circumstances – could you . . . excuse us, madam, just here, this way . . .'

With a little surge of regret she realises it is too late for a seventh option. Run off with him.

# The Secret Desire of Mervyn Smyth
## SARAH QUIGLEY

ALL HIS LIFE he had wanted a Fender Rhodes piano. While other children asked for rollerblades and Super Nintendoes, he asked for a Fender Rhodes. Every birthday and every Christmas he would write it on his list, Fender Rhodes Piano, just like that. Or FR Piano, or FRP. His parents stopped seeing it after a while, they just looked at #2 automatically. FRP could have been a part of any old list.

Pay milkman FRP Put rubbish out
Teabags Washing Powder FRP Baked Beans

So he never got his heart's desire.

Herbie Hancock was his favourite. He had fifty-four tapes, but Herbie was the best. The Fender Rhodes sang like a lark behind the rasping sax. Why can't you listen to Billie Holiday? his mother would say. Why can't you play Billie Holiday or Louis Armstrong? she'd cry, as the fringed lightshade jived to the mad bad beat. She was a modern mother, she liked Harry Connick Jnr, but Herbie and the Headhunters did nothing for her.

So he grew up with music in his veins and a secret in his heart. He could play Scarlatti and Mancini, could stun with Beethoven and stir with Brahms. He played Steinways and Yamahas, baby grands and honky-tonks and electronic keyboards. But he never got to play a Fender Rhodes (there were only two in Australasia). There were times when he put on an old tape patched with Sellotape, and then he would hear endless Sunday afternoons, tireless lawnmowers and talkback shows, and, soaring over both, the sublime tones of his secret passion.

One day he heard that Herbie Hancock was playing at a festival in Melbourne. So he got on the plane and flew into an orange Australian sunset. The hall was packed. He sat like a stone all night, not even his eyebrows moved. He sat perfectly still all night, and if his neighbours thought he was strange, well, he didn't care.

After the concert he walked out into the hot blue air. He walked round the back of the concert hall and straight in the door marked 'Artistes'. Easy as that. He followed kilometres of squeaking corridors to the heart of the hall, stepped out on stage, and there was his Fender Rhodes right in front of him. He sat straight down and his fingers knew the keys: of course, because they had been there a thousand times before.

It wasn't plugged in but he played anyway. First a perfectly executed, perfectly silent Bach sonata; and then a soundlessly triumphant 'Battle Hymn of the Republic'; and after that he just jammed.

He was caught, after what might have been half an hour, or a night or a day. He was taken away to the police station, where they quizzed him in twangy guitar accents and put him in a cell. His fingerprints left the police files spangled with Fender Rhodes dust; their luminosity had startled the sergeant.

Next day he was sent back to New Zealand. He had a record now, and whenever he went anywhere the Customs people searched his bags.

But he thought it had been worth it.

# *Redecorating*
## JANETTE SINCLAIR

IT WAS THE first anniversary of Jeannie's leaving Karl, and Cass's husband was gone to Australia for a weekend conference. 'We're painting the town tonight,' they told everyone at the office. They left the Friday drinks crowd at the Red Horse after one orange-juice-and-vodka each. Then, high on the rainbow of promise held out by the evening, they began the walk along the Golden Mile.

At 10.38 p.m. they synchronised their watches and tidied the plot as they shared a taxi to their homes in the dark suburbs.

'How was your Friday night?' The chorus at morning tea on Monday was unrelenting. Cass, groaning and clutching her temples: 'A night to remember, only I can't . . .'

'Ooh, I can,' said Jeannie. 'We went to Jack Cunneen's and drank green Guinness in goblets. On to the Underworld, and then the Mustard Gas Grill for some of the live blues Cass was hanging out for. Her eyes lit on a young black guy sitting listening; she said, 'I bet he's a Yankee soldier, look at his beautifully polished shoes.' But he turned out to be French-speaking from one of those colonies in West Africa, and he was going off to a tango class. Cass said, 'I've always wanted to learn,' and he said, 'Come avec moi, madame. It takes two.' Well, I didn't need him to tell me three's a crowd so I took off and made it home before I turned into a pumpkin.'

'Ah, it's coming back to me now,' said Cass. 'But you forgot the Sushi Bar. Jeannie had a yen for sushi, sake, the whole Floating World . . . So we tried a bit of everything going round. But she kept saying there must be more to it than this. Finally we found a place called the Indigo Kimono. Some Japanese businessman here for a conference latched on to Jeannie, started writing haiku in violet highlighter on her shirt. Last thing I saw he was teaching her to make origami condoms out of rice paper . . . Blow that, I said to myself. I mean who at two thirty in the morning needs intellectual wanking games?'

Cass winked at their circle of listeners. 'A case of selective amnesia?'

'Well, that's your story,' said Jeannie, smiling archly. 'I think I'll stick to mine.'

# *A Family Funeral*
## KEVIN IRELAND

UNCLE WARREN, MY mother's only brother, was buried last week. It was a small and sober affair, for he was a small and sober man.

'Warren would have appreciated the religious solemnity,' my mother announced in disappointment after the few mourners had gone. 'I suppose that would have to count as some sort of consolation.'

But she had never expected a crowd to turn up. What she was referring to obliquely was that only one man from his office had bothered to come, even though I pointed out in all fairness that Warren had offended most of the people who worked under him by spouting the Scriptures at them at every opportunity, and anyway he'd retired so long ago that the people he'd known would've packed up ages ago.

'They forget you that quick these days,' my mother insisted. 'I would have liked a bit less of the chapters and verses and a bit more notice taken of his achievements. That was one thing no one could dispute – for all his faults, God bless him, my brother was a very big fish in a small pool once upon a time.'

That was going too far. All day Dad had kept his trap shut. But now we'd closed the front door on what he called 'the last straggling, scone-gnawing, tea-snuffling wowser', he was into the beer at last and he wasn't in the mood for any more of the drivel. He'd held himself in too long. He snapped back, 'Come off it, Mum. You know bloody well he was called Porky behind his back. He was no fish, big or small – he couldn't swim.'

Which was the way the subject of the *Wahine* was brought up at last. The embarrassing thing that no one had mentioned all through the funeral and after was how Uncle Warren had survived when the *Wahine* hit Barrett's Reef, in 1968, and fifty-one people were drowned.

Hurricane-force winds had whipped up monster waves. It was Wellington's worst storm in living memory. But one minute my mother's brother is screaming out that he can't swim to save himself, while he's trying to shove and claw his way onto one of the three lifeboats, and the next he's standing on a small stretch of sand, brushing the spray off his lapels.

He's clutching his satchel and his office papers are dry.

'Miracle Man', Dad said contemptuously, repeating the headlines of the time. 'Funny how he pulled his little pink snout in when he saw how everyone didn't believe the baloney. I'll always wonder how he worked that stunt.'

'Do you really think he could've walked on water?' my mother asked me, looking anxiously over her shoulder.

'Uncle Warren?' I replied truthfully. 'The truth was buried with him. It'll always be a mystery.'

To which I distinctly heard Dad add, in a whisper so quiet I could only just hear him, 'Wake your ideas up, boy. Didn't you ever hear how pigs can fly?'

# The Battery Hens
## GRAEME FOSTER

HE IS GLAD to be back in work. Briskly he scuffs the square-mouth shovel across the concrete aisle and jerks the collected bird droppings back upon the heaps to the side. The hens flare.

It starts with those closest: a shrill cackle, flap of wings, rapid ruffle of rust-red feathers, the heads cocking on scrawny necks, springing like jack-in-the-boxes through wire bars, the tiny sparkling circles of their orange-brown eyes wide and wildly peering. It is contagious, explosive: three ruffling, squawking hens per cage; seventy-five chain-reacting cages per row; four rattling rows suspended over miniature mountain chains of choking droppings. A grand total of nine hundred flapping fowls in one thick Hiroshima wind.

When the pandemonium subsides, the cackle to a croon like croaking frogs, Colin rests his shovel on a feed tray and quietly slips through the laden air back to the big double doors. He leans on a door post, inhaling the humid summer air instead. And studies the door chart, the daily records of eggs collected: Monday 482, Tuesday 529, Wednesday 666.

Does Mrs Brown or Mrs Jones know when reaching for their weekly dozen in the supermarket that this is where they are collected?

As Mrs Rose Jones comes into focus, taking the weight of her carton, Colin notices she seems faint – she has leant upon her trolley. Perhaps she has been granted insight – like that gained from the lights in the egg-sorting room – and been shocked to see the eggs' pallid centres. Or is she suffering from the regular consumption of their undernourished yolks and albumens?

Strangely, her grooming, the back-combing of her red-rinsed hair, has caused it all to rise in a ridge. And now she is climbing into her trolley and, clattering and scratching, is perching on the wire frame, rearing up and down in knee-bending exercises, in soprano cackling to the supermarket's soothing orchestral melody. And at once all the housewives in Row A, the Roses and Roseannes and Rosemaries, climb into their trolleys too, breaking forth in crackling soprano or contralto, arms flailing, their rouge-red faces on long necks rising to hit the high notes, subsiding on the low.

The trolleys roll on. Round to Aisle B. And on. Passing in total four rows of items; seventy-five items per row; an average three brands per item – a grand total of nine hundred products.

They queue at the counter. Colin leans forward to peer over the shoulder of the checkout operator. It is true, the dollars and cents signs on the monitor have been replaced with egg-token symbols. Alongside are daily print-outs, tallies of tokens received: Monday 546, Tuesday 592, Wednesday 666.

It is the last figure he finds most disturbing. He mutters it over. Isn't it the Mark of the Beast?

As the sun beats harshly on the back of his head, he staggers to the egg-sorting room to give notice.

# The Looming
## PAULINE HUMPHRIES

'MR METCALF, DO you have to lean across my desk like that?'

Placing his hands flat on her desk for support, Mr Metcalf leaned his tall body even further towards her.

'Jennifer, are you sure you're all right?' he demanded, frowning, his bushy eyebrows inches from her face. She made no reply. After a minute he straightened up and walked away, glancing at Jennifer over his shoulder, still frowning.

At lunchtime Jennifer bought several tall pot plants and placed them along the edge of the L-shaped desk where Mr Metcalf usually leaned. That afternoon he hesitated by the pot plants, then walked round her desk and stood behind her chair, looming closer than ever. Jennifer moved her chair back suddenly, hoping a castor would go over his foot. Just because she was his personal assistant didn't mean he could invade her space. The castor missed his foot.

She removed the pot plants, but the pattern had been set. Mr Metcalf now sometimes loomed over her desk, and sometimes, even closer, behind her chair.

Wondering if she was exaggerating the problem, Jennifer decided to keep a record of his loomings for three months. Using her computer, she designed a chart with the dates of working days at the top of each column, and attached it to the wall. From then on, whenever Mr Metcalf loomed over her desk she added a D to that day's column, and if he loomed over her chair, she wrote in a C.

By the third day she could see an interesting pattern. More C looms took place in the mornings, the majority of Ds occurred in the afternoons. After a week she totalled and averaged the Ds and Cs. She resolved to plot a graph of them at the end of each month.

Halfway through the second week, mid-loom (a C), Mr Metcalf pointed to Jennifer's wall chart.

'What's this, Jennifer?'

'Oh, that's personal, Mr Metcalf.'

The next time he loomed, Jennifer didn't wait until he had gone before filling in her chart. She quickly wrote in a D, then faced him, with her best efficient smile, and said, 'Can I help you with something, Mr Metcalf?' He frowned, then gave her a tape of dictation for word-processing. From then on she always added to the chart while he loomed. Mr Metcalf often looked intently at it, but said nothing.

Fewer Ds and Cs took place during the last two weeks of the first month. Jennifer blu-tacked the monthly line-graph onto her wall next to the chart. During the second month there were a few looms at the beginning but none by the third week. She plotted another line-graph anyway, and added it to the wall.

For the third month there were no looms to graph. Jennifer felt almost disappointed. She brightened when she noticed Mr Metcalf picking his nose.

# *Once*
## FIONA FARRELL

ONCE, A BIRD landed on a fence post. It was a bird like no other bird. Its feathers gleamed like burnished steel and it stood on the post (which was indeed like no other post, being arthriticky, grey and bearded with tufts of pale lichen) and it sang, 'This is my post. This is my valley. This is my place.'

Once, a worm nudged blindly at damp earth. It was a worm like no other worm. Its skin was crimson silk and it rippled round the smooth curving of a buried stone.

Once, there was a woodcutter. He was chopping kanuka into even lengths for the fire and piling the pieces in a Lux Liquid carton, which was like no other carton, being buckled at one corner and lined with the 6 September edition of the Christchurch *Press*. The woodcutter was like no other. Five foot eight with shoulders shiny with sweat, jeans slung round his hips, his hair tousled.

Once, there was a little old woman who dug up treasure in her garden. It was a stone, and though it looked at first sight like all the other stones which had been borne by the river from the far mountains to just this place, beneath the bean patch, it was indeed like no other stone. The little old woman picked it up and the worm fell to the ground. The little old woman rubbed the stone and the worm flicked its crimson tail and slid down into the cool dark. She rubbed the stone a second time and the bird sang, 'This is my place. This is my place.' She rubbed it once more and this time the sun surfed out from behind the hill on a high billow of cloud, the woodcutter began to whistle 'Livin' Doll', the beans grew, the river ran, the bird sang, the worm rippled and the little old woman knew that this was indeed ever after and the time to be happy.

And she was.

# Annual Lies (Mincey Pies)
## MARIE DUNCAN

Dear Fleur,

You will see my Christmas letter has undergone a radical change. I am tired of sanitising my life, so here are a few details of what really happened this year.

Our dog died. The kids were upset but I was relieved as he had been peeing everywhere. The house still smells, but we'll get new carpet once we've paid off the credit cards.

Emily had another bad year at school. She is basically quite stupid and we see her as being virtually unemployable. Dermot is an unpleasant, sullen boy and as I can't think of one good thing to say about him, I won't even try. Jane has, after what seems like an eternity searching for something meaningful, found God.

Bryan is now quite bald, wears bifocals and constantly worries about redundancy. My work remains as boring and mundane as ever. We have decided to stay home this summer as we can't afford a holiday and painting the house has become our number one priority. The purple with forest-green trim of the eighties was a big mistake.

Have a nice Christmas.

Love
Fenella

Dear Fenella,

I am sorry if you find this letter offensive but I'm tired of your annual gushing letter. To date it hasn't arrived, but I know exactly what it will contain – very little truth.

Fenella, everyone knows Bryan is strictly lower management and that he has been very fortunate in not being made redundant. Have you considered it may be the good will of old friends which keeps him employed? Regarding your own work. I know you work for a mediocre firm and your continual talk of promotions and a demanding work-load makes me despair.

As for your children. I know Jane is living in a fundamentalist Christian community, and while I'm sure this is a great relief to you after her Sydney debacle, a little honesty on your part during her troubled times would have been appreciated.

I have two nephews at the same school as Dermot and I am appalled at what they have told me about him. It seems unbelievable that you could have ever boasted about his successful endeavours in the sporting and academic areas. We are also aware that Emily is not as talented as you have indicated.

You used to be such an honest person. Don't you realise your friends would care for you no matter what? There has never been any need for you to create such a false impression. It has made things very difficult for everyone. You have forced me to be party to your fabrications and it simply isn't good enough. You may have deceived yourself, but you have not deceived me. I find the last few years' annual lies are simply too hard to bear. I think it would be better if we ceased to correspond.

Yours
Fleur

# A Chance Encounter
## TIM HIGHAM

JENNY WORKED FOR an ear, nose and throat specialist.

But it was her ears and nose that interested me. The ear lobes were generous and the nose was slightly hawkish.

The first time I lay near her she moaned and mumbled in a way that has become familiar. Then, though, we were separated by the polished floors of a hospital ward and incapable of closing the distance.

We were admitted on the same day, but she wouldn't have known that. It took her a few days to come around.

As her internal injuries healed, I began slipping under the blanket, murmuring around the ears and tracing the curve of her nose with my own.

She was discharged before me but kept visiting and then we started spending weekends together.

We probably looked a little strange, a fifty-something practice manager and a limping, leather-jacketed man half her age. She'd angle her walk into me on the way to our favourite deli to mull over cappuccinos and the papers. I got dragged into all sorts of shops: after literary magazines, opera CDs, designer kitchenware. Even into a changing cubicle to find the outfit and every other item of clothing on the chair.

The relationship was always on her terms. I wouldn't see her through the week, then for two days cruise shops and bars, and tumble back to her flat. I went along for the ride, not asking questions. But there were a few secrets I kept to myself too.

I'd been working at Canterbury Motorcycles and doing well. Had the knack of spotting a willing buyer as soon as he walked into the yard. I could tell those that never intended paying more than the deposit; they always wanted a big bike, something over 500 cc.

Six weeks after the second payment hadn't come through we'd chase them up. I got on well with the repossession guy and used to ride with him. I guess that's where I got the bug.

It was a big Ducatti parked on the porch of an old plaster house on the Avon Loop. I stood under a hedge for three nights, worked out how to run it onto grass in the middle of a gravel driveway with a length of timber.

I heard the sirens before I was even two blocks away. A neighbour having a spa by candlelight in the townhouse next door watched everything.

I thought I could outrun them. Killed the lights and roared alongside the river. Out of the shadow of the willows and into the avenue's street lights and six lanes.

Having made five, I thought I'd squeeze past that last car. Its driver never saw the Ducatti till it was buckling the door panel.

As I sailed over the bonnet, eyes rolled up to meet mine, the moment freeze-framed by adrenaline. Zigzag silver earrings swinging wildly on those lobes, nostrils flaring with pain as the inside door handle rode up into her abdomen.

# The Falling Game
## GWENYTH PERRY

WHO, AFTER ALL, is this man sitting lunching with me, in this French provincial town with the crooked cathedral by the tree-lined river?

The waiter has taken us for English.

'You come for our lovely weather,' he says firmly.

'Yes,' I reply in French. 'But at home in New Zealand we have good weather too.'

'Ah, New Zealand. *Rainbow Warrior*. We do not agree, our government was bad.'

He beams his friendship.

'What a fuss about a boat.'

'A man died.'

'Men die every minute.'

What am I doing here with him?

I watch old men playing boules under plane trees in the square. Dessert arrives. I talk about our superb meal, duck as only the French can cook it, tarts, apples, Normandy, waving my hands about as usual. He scorns my imperfect French, correcting me frequently. His French is perfect, precise, too correct, like his lovemaking. I'm usually clumsy, the first to trip and fall, in life and language.

My last gesture catches the side of my glass. I freeze as red wine splashes across the paper cloth, which absorbs none of it, pouring whole into his lap and dripping to the floor.

He stops. He has class. Not a word of reproach. Expression quickly controlled. He gets up and walks to the wash-room, dabbing ineffectually with his napkin. I watch the waiter mopping up, righting the glass. As I start grinning he winks at me. Realisation dawns. I'm free.

He'll be pleased to see the back of this mad colonial now. No regrets. Fall in easily, fall out just as easily. I order coffee from the discreetly grinning waiter; only French waiters can grin discreetly. I put my sugar cubes with his to give him an extra boost.

After a long time he returns, shirt clinging wetly; he must have taken it off to wash. He sits gingerly, a long way from the table. I feel a twinge of remorse as I see the pink stain on his tan pants, now stuck to the curve of that delectable tight bum I have just renounced.

'I think I'll head for the mountains now,' he says. It is nearly a question.

'I'd rather go to the coast. It's getting a bit claustrophobic inland all the time.' He winces in appreciation of my choice of words.

We stay agreeable, make polite farewells, say take care, stay in touch, don't fall off the edge of the world, it's been good.

I leave him sitting with more coffee. I'm out of sight when I fall down the cafe steps, my knees weak with relief and laughter. Only the waiter sees, his expressive dark eyes showing how he, too, would like to fall about laughing.

# Ghosts in the Garden
## VICTORIA FELTHAM

'MUSICALS NEED CHORUSES,' I told Lulu when she blanched at the array of ghosts in The Secret Garden. 'You can't compose a musical by threading solos and duets together like beads on a string. You need crowds.'

Privately I agreed with her. Why did they have to litter The Secret Garden with ghosts? Virtually every scene, in the garden or out of it, bristled with them. Not just Colin's dead mother, a major character, and ubiquitous, but also Mary's dead parents. And their contemporaries.

From start to finish, officers of the Raj, in dress uniform, and their dazzling wives by the ballroomful, waltzed towards the cholera which orphaned Mary. Ghosts outnumbered people. Even during the final scene, in the garden, the nostalgic throngs of partying dead effectively submerged the book's message of rebirth.

Lulu's hand seized mine in the opening dream scene and kept it, except when she went to buy an ice cream. She's been very clingy this last year, so I worried when the ghosts were moonlit even during the daytime scenes. Lulu hates moonlight. The full moon, leering through her bedroom window, terrified her when she was little. She'd scream from behind her hands for me to pull her curtains. Soupy assurances ('Here's Lulu's friend, the moon. Hello, moon.') cut no ice at all.

Still, after the show she reckoned she'd adored it. I was the one feeling ghastly.

I told myself the show was execrable, a travesty of the book, which leaves you free to create whatever number of spirits you can tolerate, out of one spoken message: 'Archie! Archie! In the garden.' But calling the show bad didn't counter its effects.

The following week, cowed by headaches and nausea, I was plagued by the conviction that I was soon to be a solicitous ghost myself, ballroom dancing through the rest of Lulu's childhood.

'I feel really weird,' I confessed.

'Ugh, don't say that, Mummy,' she recoiled, then stationed a Sylvanian kitten in its cradle. 'Remember Callum Stuart in J1? His grandfather said he wasn't feeling good, went to bed early, and never woke up.'

That did it. Seeing white feathers on the doorstep, I caved in and went to the doctor.

'Don't laugh, but . . .' I explained. She gave me a thorough checkup and a lab request form for every known blood test.

Then the Dunedin funeral director wrote to ask did I still intend to bury Mother's ashes in the Cathedral rose garden? The first anniversary had passed . . .

My reply was crabby: I wasn't dragging the chain. That garden had been dismantled for a year while they rebuilt its retaining wall. And yes, I'd fly down, with Lulu. Who wouldn't let me vanish to Dunedin without her. We'd bury her grandmother's ashes together.

Writing the letter cured me.

And the blood tests came back normal, too.

# *Sleeping with the Phone*
## DIANE BROWN

AT THE PUB the poet says he can come to no firm conclusions about phone sex, but this man I am calling long distance at night rates was born in Los Angeles and has no such inhibitions.

I grew up in Grey Lynn. My parents were atheists and proud of their heathenism. It is possible for me to lie naked under the sun all day, letting the fingers of a lover drip juice into my mouth. My mother, however, had some empathy with Patricia Bartlett and would never allow me to play with myself 'down there'.

My father was more relaxed about sexual desires. 'Like him, obsessed with sex,' my mother said. I'm not sure if Social Welfare would approve either. I cannot remember if they have a policy on sleeping with the phone. More importantly, is there an emergency benefit for toll calls? The office is closed at nights so I tell the American I can only afford five minutes.

He says I need to admit to my desires. If I ask nicely he will ring back after he has fed his dog. His voice slides down my throat and I am a little girl at the sweets counter, tongue hanging out. 'Please,' I say. Even heathens know their manners. He does ring back and when he asks what I am wearing, I do not tell him about the blue winceyette pyjamas with the pink appliqued kitten. It helps to be a writer who lies. In bed wearing a black satin negligee. Sheer lace down to the waist.

He tells me he is planning to uncover every inch of my body. I am thankful it is dark. He cannot see the stretch marks and my cellulite thighs. And his teeth nibbling my toes are soon lips licking my nipples.

In this environment sound is what matters most. How to simulate. I have had no rehearsal, but I breathe loudly in harmony with his increasing rhythm. I hope my son in the next room is asleep. He is learning CPR and may get the wrong idea.

Once I had an orgasm on a bus, but I was wearing tight jeans and the road was full of potholes. The lover sitting next to me was asleep at the time. He was upset with the realisation that he might be redundant. He said I must have been dreaming.

Tonight I have a foreign voice interfering with my imagination. For a while it is enough. Then I open my eyes and discover I want to embrace reality. To feel the facts of another body. My arms reach upwards and pass clean through the cold black air.

Like the poet I have not come to any firm conclusions about phone sex.

# *Maternity*
## RHONDA BARTLE

DAVID'S MOTHER ALWAYS managed somehow to upset her. There was the time Vaddi had arrived, face aglow, screeching. 'Where's Our Lovely Little Mother-To-Be? I have a present for Our Baby!' And there, lying like a shroud, layered in tissue, was the most extraordinary jacket. It was made of virgin lambswool, soft and gentle as snow falling, thousands of perfect white puff-balls, held together with needle and floss. It was lined with satin of an immediate match, and five mother-of-pearl buttons went eagerly down its substantial front. Angel Garb. Downy and fresh.

Elizabeth watched dollar signs flashing neon, on, off, on, off. The label read 'Birth to Three Months. Dryclean Only.'

'Take it back,' Elizabeth spat. Oh, Vaddi meant well of course.

'Take it back and swap it,' hissed Elizabeth under her breath. 'For three dozen nappies, ten packets of soap powder, a truckful of sanitary pads for later. Anything.'

She thought, bloody Vaddi.

A third-generation Kiwi with that dumb, foreign-sounding name, and where David had got his from – the number of times she had heard that. 'I named him after me,' said Vaddi. 'You know, you just change the letters around. Clever eh!'

Clever all right. To bring this expensive, useless thing for this baby, to hang it in the doorway of this forlorn little room, with its no curtains, no lightshades, bare bulbs dangling, no floormats. Oh – but she nearly forgot. Carpet had been put down in their bedroom, a beautifying bit of Bremworth with its ribald pattern rooted forever to the corridor between bed and wall, down all three sides. It was studded with tacks, their silly shiny faces winking stupidly in the sunlight.

'Bare boards!' Vaddi had thrown up her hands in dramatic horror. 'We must do something about this.'

'I like the boards,' said Elizabeth gently. 'I like the way they warm up in the morning. When I sweep, sand falls down the cracks and heads back to the beach.' She imagined each individual grain rolling gleefully back home, back to Mum and Dad and the rest of the family. The floor was the colour of the driftwood half buried on the sand bank.

'I like it like this,' said Elizabeth.

But there came a day when Vaddi appeared with a syrup tin of tacks, trusty hammer and a face ossified with intent.

'I'm here about the floor,' she announced. She set about changing the landscape of the room forever, down on chubby knees with her broad bum in the air. Tacking, tacky, tack. The carpet had lain down and died there. And Elizabeth, at her uncharitable best, could just hear Vaddi after her next conquering round of golf.

'The newlyweds? How nice of you to ask. Yes, they're doing quite nicely. We just carpeted their bedroom you know.'

# Growing Pain
## DAWN SHEPPARD

BETH KNEW WHEN her sense of unease began. She had watched as the train pulled out of the little siding and the guard's van rounded the bend beside the bush-lined river. It was after 9 p.m. but the long southern twilight still held.

All became quiet and she was alone. Her mother should have stepped off the train in her neat navy-blue coat, carrying the big zipped leather bag. The Christmas treats would be in it, bought during the day-long shopping in town. The tingling anticipation had gone, deadened by the strange emptiness settling inside her.

Beth walked hesitantly into the warm kitchen. The kettle was boiling on the wood range and she had earlier set the table for supper. Her father was already sitting there, reading the paper, slippers on, braces with Fire and Police stamped on the metal fasteners, showing over his work shirt. She wished sometimes that he would wear belts like the younger fathers.

'She didn't come. She must have missed the train.'

He said nothing, just shrugged and turned the page. But he wasn't reading, she could tell. Confused and anxious, Beth carefully made the tea.

'I don't feel like tea tonight, Beth. Just you get off to bed now – your mother will be home on tomorrow's train. Don't you worry about her. She's all right.'

Next day was the school picnic at the beach. All the mothers would be there, very few fathers, working away at the sawmills or on their farms. There were the sports for the children, and the mothers' race. Every year Beth could remember, she had thrilled to see her young, pretty mother flash past the other puffing, giggling ones with their flabby, knotted legs. Then they would all sit down in the sand at the edge of the bush for the annual prizegiving. Everyone received something. Beth's was for General Excellence, not just Neatness or Helpfulness. Mother and daughter shared their triumphs.

But this day's pleasure had disappeared, dull like the ache she felt somewhere near her throat. The mothers' race was won by Mrs Parker, who fell over at the tape and showed her underwear. And Mrs Gallagher and Mrs Parker had looked at each other with tight little smiles when she told them her mother had missed the train the previous night.

Her mother was there of course when she got home. She was standing at the sink peeling potatoes. Yes, she had missed the train and stayed at a private hotel. She did not even ask about the picnic.

Beth went out to the calf paddock, where her father was fencing. He rammed the earth fiercely and sweat ran down his face in big drops. Once he looked towards the house and Beth was aware of the puzzled misery in his eyes and, again, that shrug.

Beth knew that night and day had been the beginning of real pain, years of it, for all of them.

# The Bank Job
## JOHN C. ROSS

HANGING AROUND, TO get the timing right, was the worst part, with Patrick and Patrick in their black cassocks strolling up and down the centre aisle of the nearest church, drawing gossip out of its priest. The three nuns knelt, wandered about mumbling to each other.

In the bank, things happened quickly. One moment the teller with the scarlet Father Christmas hat was enjoying a bit of backchat with the priest with the white quiff in his hair, the next she was staring up the nostril of his handgun. She saw another priest holding up Bernadette on her left, and two nuns, pistols held two-handed, yelling at the customers, 'Lie down flat, will yezz, like sensible people now, and nobody will get herrt!'

So close to Christmas they had plenty of cash already bagged up, bulked out with holiday pay, for the armoured van crew to pick up and take round to the local brewery ten minutes later.

Outside, by the getaway car, the third nun spotted a Garda car in the distance, pulled a whistle from her sleeve and blew a shrill warning. Inside, the black-garbed thugs grabbed up the bags already within reach, shouted, 'A merry Christmas to yezz all,' then dashed out and away.

Within fifteen minutes the cardboard numberplates had been torn off and burnt. The weapons, wrapped in plastic, were buried deep under the weeds in the back garden. Mary, Mary, Mary, Patrick and Patrick were hugging each other in Mary O'Connor's dingy flat, then pulling off their vestments and packing up the loot.

That evening, in mufti, Mary and Mary boarded the boat from

Dunleary to Liverpool. Mary O'Connor led Patrick and Patrick, all three dressed as nuns, on to the boat for Holyhead.

Halfway across the Irish Sea an alert young English plainclothes policeman suddenly noticed one of the nuns nearby had great heavy men's shoes under her robe. And yes, a blue-tinged chin. And by God, so did the one beside her. Terrorists! IRA terrorists! A bomb outrage in London on Christmas Day! Action at once!

Thrusting his way to the bow, he tried to call up the Holyhead police with his cellphone. It took forever to get through to anyone. And then, at Holyhead, in the wee small hours, five bleary-eyed police watched in bafflement as dozens of nuns filed past them, in the crowd bustling grumpily towards the London train.

When the train at last pulled into Euston Station it was surrounded by lethally armed SAS men. Screening the passengers took hours. All the women police in the Metropolitan region were there. They conscientiously stripsearched fifty-seven enraged Irish nuns.

Meanwhile, after several discreet changes of trains and garb, Mary, Mary, Mary, Patrick and Patrick disembarked severally at Glasgow Central and made their way to Patrick's flat, making plans for the best Hogmanay ever.

# There's a Monkey in My Kitchen
## MAGGIE BARTLETT

THERE'S A MONKEY in my kitchen. I can hear it. Eating muesli. It came in not long ago from its cage: a caravan parked on a spare bit of road between here and the neighbour's. Where it spent the night of the storm.

Monkey is always angry before a storm. Before the rain that swells the river that swells the grasses that pull and tug a hole now and then, causing a slip of stones and rocks and gravel.

My belly aches, stretched tight by bars of steel argument.

There are too many storms with Monkey. Lightning flashes as thunder growls and I can't resolve the nasties we've put between us. They won't dissolve or be washed away, out into the bay with the other excesses of stones, branches, chemicals, pesticides, plastic bags and wire coathangers, violent words, threats of love and hate and I'm leaving you.

Talk doesn't come easily to Monkey. He knows the words as individuals but not in families. His grunts lose their eloquence without physical contact to transmit their meanings. Grunts are of no use in a storm, yet are adequate enough in coital positions when fur and smell are all that's needed. In the moment.

But we can't remain in coitus forever, Monkey. We must speak. Love each other with our minds as well as our bodies.

Monkey's children visit on weekends. One boy is his, the other is not – although his mother passes him off as Monkey's. She collected him when she was screwing around, trying to hurt

Monkey and herself. Then, she could not decide. Was it to be aborted? Yes? No.

There was no blood spilt. No furry, white, floating jellyfish was to be scraped from her reluctant womb because, 'The child will keep us together, Monkey,' she wailed.

'What absolute garbage!' he said. And he was right.

The child didn't keep them together because they were already broken.

Monkey needs to pretend the child is his, and so the child visits us on weekends. He shits his pants till he's six years old. He bears little or no resemblance to Monkey, but it doesn't matter, Monkey says.

'That's fine,' I scream. 'If you feed him! If you clean his shitty pants and wipe his bum!'

I try hard to accept the boy. But I can't. I see him as her kid and not yours, Monkey. I could make the effort for your sake, but your sake is being washed away in all these storms.

Give me your share of love – freely and flowing naturally, Monkey. Not a great gush and rush of stormwater love – but a constant, reliable trickle. I'd settle for a dribble and call it precious, Monkey.

No. He wants to play Hide and Seek.

'Come and get me!' Monkey says.

'No,' I say. 'It's not fair. I want a turn to hide.' And Monkey grins at my efforts to force him out to be caught. He enjoys the chase.

# The Old Woman and the Bear
## ELSPETH SANDYS

COULD IT BE her mother? Impossible surely. It would be ten years this Christmas. What would she be doing in this country anyway? There'd been no contact between them. No one from back there knew where she lived now.

She approached the figure huddled on the bed. The woman was real all right, though half dead by the look of her. A bundle of bones, with eyes like hot coals. It was the eyes she'd seen first. They'd turned on her when she came in through the door. Don't think you can escape, they signalled.

'Who are you?' the girl demanded. At which moment the ground split open beneath her and she was hurled first against the bed, then against the opposite wall.

Coming to, she heard a voice. 'You'll have a new life,' it was saying. 'You'll be safe.'

Dragging her bruised body across the floor, the girl reached the centre of the room. Beams of dusty light fell across the bed, the shelves packed with knick-knacks, the faded Indian rugs. She'd become a hoarder since she moved to this country. It was a bad habit.

As she crouched, fighting for breath, the girl tried to think what day it was. Saturday. That was it. She'd gone out to do her shopping. Had she left the door unlocked? She must have. Otherwise how could the woman have got in?

While she struggled to find answers she could feel the woman's eyes, boring into her back. She'd come in to shelter. That was the explanation. But it hadn't rained, had it? There'd been thunder, she remembered that. It had been so sudden it had winded her. But she couldn't recall rain. Rain she always associated with safety.

Moving only her eyes, the girl began to examine her possessions: the clothes on the rail; the signed photos of rock stars; the lamp she'd made out of a chianti bottle; those knick-knacks . . . 'The first thing you learn is renunciation,' she could hear her mother saying.

Suddenly everything began to sway – the clothes, the lamp, the brooding faces. Next thing she knew she'd been thrown against the bed again. The eyes smiled at her through a cloud of dust. When history and flesh and blood are one, they confirmed, there's no escape, ever.

It was then she saw the bear. He was crouched in the corner where the TV usually stood. But the set was broken. The man had come this morning to collect it. So how had the bear got in? Had he come with the woman? And what was wrong with him? His breathing was hoarse and irregular; his eyes full of blood.

The girl pushed her way to his side. Her arms reached out to him. 'Too raloo raloora,' she sang. 'Too raloo rali.'

That was when the first stone fell. It missed the girl, tumbling into the centre of the room where it lay among the rugs. Strangely, there was no sound, neither then nor later, when the stones began to fall like hail and the roof slowly crumbled in a shower of dust and plaster.

She turned to the woman, but that part of the room was lost now. 'Too raloo raloora . . .' Huge and helpless, the bear sank into her arms, squeezing the breath from her lungs, silencing her song.

When the rubble was finally cleared, a young woman (as yet unidentified) was found to be the only victim. She had died clutching a small teddy bear in her arms.

# *Bouncing*
# RICHARD BROOKE

THE LATE 1980S came up with a new way of cheating death. Bungy jumping. Those thin rubber bands tied to your ankles, leaping out into space with your heart in your mouth. Frank watched them on TV, jumping singly or in couples. Putting all their faith in those cords, the camera closing on that look of sheer disbelief as they fell down and down. This was love all right, just the way the old songs called it:

*When you and I are one*
*breath, one heart forever . . .*

Frank had recently fallen in love. One wretched, wet dog of a day, with nothing going right in the music shop where he worked, he had decided to go home early. As he crossed the road outside the mall he saw Annie struggling with parcels at the bus stop. Frank had always been attracted to the exquisite cliché, and let's face it, he had all the great song lyrics in his head, so there was a certain inevitability about their meeting.

When she suggested they do a bungy jump together, Frank was left speechless.

'I love you, Annie,' he then said lamely.

'Yes, I know. I love you too,' she replied, her mouth a perfect pout.

He could only marvel at her small, hopeful breasts under the drab olive shirt with the insignia of the German army.

'When?' he spluttered.

'Tomorrow.' She kissed him without any irony. 'It'll be awesome.'

The platform seemed to be made of ice, such was the coldness in Frank's feet, and it was spreading up around his heart. They were tied together, face to face, and as he looked into her eyes he was sure he heard music.

'Annie,' he whispered, but she wasn't listening. He felt her breath on his neck, and wondered if he was being tested in some awful, chivalric way.

They fell, and yes, it was heart-stopping stuff. Like angels in flight. Frank couldn't breathe and his arms ached. With her body pressed against his, nothing up here made any sense at all, and then they were bouncing. Back up into the white sky. Bouncing. He looked at her and saw her mouth was open and she was gasping.

'Wow.'

Her eyes were wide open too. Ecstatic.

'Wow.'

Tears stained her cheeks as they hung in the bright chill air. Frank had a sudden rush of terror. He knew it was all downhill from here. Nothing could be this good ever again. He wanted to drop into space, vanish. She would play the videotape over and over, to friends, future lovers, at endless dinner parties. To put a charge into their sex life. Even after he was dead he would be tied to her forever. His heart sank, worse than a stone.

After they were lowered to the ground she turned to him and gave him a dazzling smile.

'We should do it again.'

'You do it again and I'll watch.'

She pursed her lips.

'Which bit did you like?' she asked.

'The beginning,' Frank said.

# *Vampire Dances*
## JAN FARR

SHE HID BENEATH the bedclothes so Laura wouldn't see her cry. So hard, the young, their world all rams and bytes. No hearts — only the tick and whine of a motor warming up.

Was this her first cave? There must have been another — warm like this, filled with fluids that muffled her mother's heart; that wet her face like this — and she must have come out, blinking the dark away; sleeves rolled, hammer in one hand, sickle in the other — ready to fight the men in suits — men with briefcases stuffed full of people's lives.

There was always a poor soul, eyes drowning in pools of fear. Soft-mouthed girls who stumbled from the storeroom while the overseer wiped his hands.

And then came Robert. Robert, who blew around inside her with her breath. The very thought of him could make her dissolve — leaking her colours into the air — which may have explained the miracle of their walls — rainbows, melting from one wall to the next.

'The union's here!' Betty had said, as if introducing Satan. She'd looked up, lost in a moment, spun into the vortex of Robert's eyes.

It was a fairground ride, when she looked back — a roller coaster — studying the hidden history of the world — words written by a Vampire, in blood — *Culloden, Parihaka, Waihi, Guernica, Lidice* — luring the Vampire into the open, spotting each fresh disguise, facing him when he traced new words for the bloodied list — *Orakei Marae*, 1951, *Vietnam, Bastion Point, Moruroa* — learning to fight him and when to dance.

And now the Vampire was parading as her own grandchild. They should have driven a stake through his heart!

They had marched – multiplied like the stars after dusk – fourteen, then fifty, a hundred – thousands – shoulder to shoulder – optimism flowing between them like melted butter – banners splashing the air with scarlet slogans – their song rising over Queen Street like a flock of doves.

And somewhere past the Post Office Square, where they had laughed, unfurled banners and posed for posterity, somewhere, between the raised arms and the moving shoulders, she'd catch a glimpse of Robert's face.

It was the way Laura had said it. Standing by the bed with their book – hers and Robert's. 'Why did you fall for it, Gran? All that neo-religious crap.'

Somewhere, between the raised arms – a glimpse of his face.

Her shoulders shook. She reached out from her cave for something to cling to.

Found her grand-daughter's hand.

# The Old Man in the Hat
## PETER EDMONDS

JOE WAS OUR best rep, and good company. Irish, with an infectious sense of humour and wide interests, particularly in world travel, which he shared with his partner, Liz. Mostly they had to read about travel in books, but they had enjoyed OE and they had ambitions.

Joe worked hard, sometimes too conscientiously, leading to nervous exhaustion. His doctor and Liz suggested he take things more easily.

He enjoyed a glass but never drove after drinking. While working in Australia he had been picked up by the police driving home from a party. Out of the car, lean against it with your arms on the roof, frisked like a common criminal, over the limit, hand over your keys, locked up for the night, up before the beak next morning, heavy fine, lucky not to lose your licence and your job.

So whenever we had an office party, Joe would go home, change and come by taxi. He did the same for functions at his club.

One thing that bugged Joe was having to drive from Auckland to Hamilton in a hurry to keep a last-minute appointment at our Hamilton office. The *AA Road Atlas* suggests a time of two hours and ten. Our boss said he could do it one hour fifteen, but he had a cousin who was a traffic cop in Huntly and knew when they had their meal breaks. He just put his foot down, the boss said.

Joe said that whenever he was in a hurry he would come across an early-model car being driven in the middle of the road at fifty k an hour by an old man in a hat, a retired cow cocky taking Mum shopping in Huntly.

Liz had finally persuaded Joe to take an overseas holiday, to Italy, where they would visit every Roman site, every opera house and picture gallery from Capri to Venice. Joe thought a few more beaches to lounge on would be good, but he was looking forward to the adventure.

He was making one last trip to Hamilton when he encountered the old man in the hat. A line of vehicles piled up behind Joe until, uncharacteristically, he overtook, ignoring the rugby-field rule. A logging truck was coming the other way. From the traffic behind, the last that was seen of Joe was careering off to the right into the Waikato River.

You might think that was the end of Joe. But, the luck of the Irish. The car was a write-off, but he walked from it unscathed.

Our boss wasn't impressed but agreed that Joe needed that holiday.

So Joe and Liz took off for Italy. That was a wonderful summer and they did it all. Until they were dining in Florence, when Joe collapsed and died.

Before they had left Auckland, Joe had shown their itinerary to our boss.

'That,' he said, 'will make you a candidate for a coronary.'

# *Dragging It*
## FRANCES CHERRY

'I'M TOTALLY DEVOTED to you,' he sings as he finishes attaching his false eyelashes. The face stares back at him out of the mirror, aloof, beautiful, scarlet lips pouting. 'No doubt about it, Virginia,' he says, 'you're a knockout.' She raises an eyebrow, mocking him. 'Come on,' he says. 'Lighten up a little.' She turns away and then looks back at him over her shoulder. Miss Untouchable Cool. He examines her from head to foot. That silver lamé covers her like the skin of a sinuous snake. Now for the silver earrings. He feels around in his flax kete until he finds the long dangling slivers of silver, tinkling and shivering as he puts them on. She steps back from the mirror. Oh yes.

Virginia puts her hand on the bed as she slips on her silver high heels. As she stalks out of the room she kicks his greasy, oil-stained jeans under the bed, feels her nose quiver. Filth. He is filth. This place is filth. There has to be something better.

The lemon meringue pie sits on the formica bench, a ghost of steam drifting upwards. He's a good cook, she has to say that for him. And then the cat, twisting itself around her legs. 'Call this devotion, do you, Marilyn?' she says. 'I know you're only after one thing.' She opens the fridge, presses her scarlet-tipped fingers to her chin in horror. Now she's going to stink of fish. Still, the cat can't starve. 'You'll have to have it on the bench tonight, darling, Mother can't bend down.'

She washes her hands with scented soap, wraps the pie in a clean tea towel, throws her silver lamé bag over her shoulder, trips along the hallway and out the door.

Along his mother's path, wild flowers and grass. Summery smells. Hoping that Dora next door is watching the television and not looking through the window. Opening the back door, shoving the pie on the bench. Calling, 'Mum, I've just left the pie. See you tomorrow.'

Pulling open the stiff door of the Hillman Avenger, fitting herself inside, arms and legs with nowhere to go. Chugging up the hill to the university.

The dykes on the door look bored as they stamp her hand. The queen at the end of the table looks at her with envy, competitiveness, something.

'Virginia,' a tentative voice says.

She turns, looks down. 'Sheree, darling, you look wonderful.' Blonde, glistening, dewy red lips.

'Not a patch on you,' Sheree giggles. 'For a moment I thought I'd made a mistake.'

'My best creation yet,' she says. 'Even if I do say it myself.'

Faces look up at her as she sweeps through preening colourful men and bland colourless women to the dance floor. Stands there, feeling all eyes upon her and then she's off. *I am woman, I am strong* . . .

# The Fear
## ROSE OMAR

YOU REMEMBER THAT day very clearly, as if it were yesterday. Yes, it was the day that the mountains changed from purple to black. At that moment everything you saw turned to black.

You woke up early and it was a bright sunny morning and the mountains reflected the light brightly upon your long flowing blonde hair as you ran up and down the long gravel driveway, chasing the butterflies and smelling the country air. Enjoying yourself as three-year-olds do.

You could see your mum busy in the kitchen, her floral pinny wrapped around her waist. She was busy preparing the food at this time of the morning. She was too busy to play with you.

So you continued to laugh, running all over the place. Around to the wooden playhouse to gather your dolls. And this morning you are going on a special outing with your 'girls'. It's going to be lots of fun for all of you as you make the long trek down to the mailbox. And even better still, your mum is going to come with you. You know it's going to be lots of fun, as it's one of your favourite games.

There's your mum, still wearing her floral pinny. You race over to her eagerly and start the 'journey'.

Your game's fully in play and you notice the sweet-smelling flowers begin to smell sickly as you feel the fear. Your heart is beating rapidly. A chill sweeps through your body and you see the still figure of the woman at the fence, yelling, '*I'm gonna kill you.*'

You feel terrified at seeing her gun pointed in your face, as the fear begins to eat you, clutching your throat as if to strangle you.

Your voice has vanished, as has your saliva. Your hand tightens on your mum's as you vaguely hear her voice reasoning with the mad woman whose face has become distorted.

Your fear continues and you vaguely see the 'people' trying to calm you down, but you can't even remember their names or faces. The only thing you feel is fear. Even after the long wait you had for your grandparents to come and collect you, you still know no peace. And on the long journey to their home you still think that woman will kill you.

The ensuing months are long and dark away from your home and the sun no longer seems as bright to you. You and the 'girls' don't like to play the mailbox game any more.

And sometimes even now, in the dark or on one of those elusive moments, the fear returns, and you can see the gun barrel pointing in your face with the faceless woman in black.

# Bob Marley in Red
## ROSS LAY

IT'S THURSDAY AND you're over at the Rising Sun. Stagnant streams of traffic snake beneath you in every direction. 'Drive Time', radio programmers call it, optimistically. A cold jug dribbles slowly onto your pitted table top and the chick in the red dress is one ball away from winning another game.

Aretha takes over the jukebox, whipping a couple of black-leather queens into a frenzy by the bar.

*You make me feel like a Nat-Tu-Ral womaaaaan.*

You guide the pale yellow coin into chrome and push till the balls roll noisily into sight. Triangle. Eighteen-weight cue. Chalk. The break's good: unders are always lucky. Ron pats you on the back as he heads for a urinal. You quickly pot two more balls and while you're walking back to your glass, Bob Marley comes over the speakers. You know it's a sign.

*Rise up dis mornin', smile wit' da rising sun . . .*

Someone at the next table waves a spliff in your face and those headlights out across the harbour become a vast illuminated pattern, created solely for your individual pleasure. The chick in the red dress doubles her yellow into one of the centre pockets and flashes you a smile.

*Sweet songs of melodies pure an' true . . .*

She rests the cue across her shoulders, leans back and starts to sway. The words glide effortlessly from her lips and you know she's not faking; she is Bob Marley. For a moment it's August school holidays 1978 and you're part of the mesmerised crowd at Western Springs. Black Power banners and suburban white kids. Bob looks your way and it's the single greatest moment of your teenage life.

*Every li'l thing's gonna be alrighhh* . . .

The song fades as the black ball glides gently into the top corner pocket. You navigate a half-circle round the table and briefly but warmly shake her hand.

'Nice game,' you offer, and mean it.


The next couple of hours dissolve into a reassuring haze of beer, more pool and instantly forgotten arguments. At some stage the cops drag off old Tommy. He's back before closing and the barman shouts him a jug, but you can see he's shaken.

As you push through the doors a blast of cold clean air catches at your lungs. You exhale noisily and head in the general direction of home. The streams of rush-hour traffic have just about dried up, but there's still a steady trickle of single men cruising the darkened streets in family cars.

Among the shadows of Edinburgh Street you recognise the red dress. She's thrown a jacket over it but must still be cold. You think about turning back but know it's too late. She's leaning back against a wall, but it's more than just the absence of a pool cue that alters everything. Bob Marley's dead and this time you're dreading her smile.

# *Sam, a Study*
## MARTHA MORSETH

SHE SAT AT her desk with a hole punch, punching hole after hole, taking five sheets of refill at a time. The girl next to her watched the white circles falling on the desk. Sam ignored her and kept punching more holes.

The girl leaned closer and blew, moving the circles. Then the girl across the aisle from Sam looked up. Sam kept punching. Sensing activity behind her, the girl in front turned round and started blowing. White circles scattered across Sam's desk and into Sam's lap and onto the floor. Everyone stopped working. They were all blowing.

Like a snake striking, Sam leapt up and hit the girl beside her with the metal punch, then went for the girl in front. There was yelling and confusion, and Sam took up her books and stomped out of the room, pushing aside the teacher from the classroom next door who had come to see why the unsupervised study group had erupted.

Peeling an orange was an art that Sam had perfected. Not for her was the use of a table knife like they had been taught in Home Ec. As if using a knife on an orange would keep her from getting fucked by life, or even just fucked. Knives were better saved for taking care of blokes.

Sam began by biting the stem part, nice and deep so that part of the middle pith came out. Then, with her fingernails, she peeled from right to left. Perfect, except when the skin stuck to the segments and juice trickled down her arm. But today the orange was yielding, her fingers dextrous, and her friend, who leaned on the second-floor balcony with Sam, was properly impressed.

The two of them watched their peelings fall to the street below. A lunch-duty teacher from a classroom below also watched the peelings fall.

'Fucking slag, mind your own business,' got Sam a week's detention and her mother an afternoon from work to see the principal. 'God, you'd think I threw the slut over the balcony,' Sam told her counsellor, who was not as sympathetic as usual. She placed a contract in front of Sam. No harassment from teachers in exchange for proper behaviour. Sure, she'd sign. No skin off her nose and it might get a few people off her back.

The day she brought the dope was a bad day. One of the turds saw her passing a joint and ratted to the principal. She was out. Expelled. There'd be conferences, a psychiatrist maybe. At least she didn't have a father to contend with, not after her mother threw the bastard out.

She could handle her mother, calm her down with a bit of housework, get a meal or two, for a while anyway. Then she was out of there. As soon as she scored some dak and was able to unload it, she'd be away. Maybe Wellington or Auckland. That was where it was happening; that was where Sam was meant to be.

# *Bondi*
## SIMON ROBINSON

THERE IT IS, slung between two rocky headlands, that lazy sweep of sand: Bondi. On the main road a kid illegally parks a 750 cc Honda motorbike, its Learner plates carefully obscured by the mudguard. An actor, well he would be if only someone would give him a break, is serving pasta in the corner café. A woman, green taffeta flailing, runs across the road to greet her lover.

The white sandy ribbon radiates the day's heat, warming the air, loosening tongues.

People gabble and chatter. The shops hum. Inside a Turkish restaurant friends are singing Happy Birthday. The birthday boy slumps forward on to his plate. He's been drinking, for he's a jolly good fellow, since eleven o'clock that morning.

At the Bondi Pavilion two men secure a red carpet outside the main door. Some scruffy boys start to enter. 'It's closed,' says the doorman.

'Why?'

'It's past five o'clock. Come back tomorrow.'

'What is it?'

'A fashion show.'

'Why aren't you inside looking at all the sheilas?'

'It's been on for days. I'm tired of it.'

A bus lurches to a halt and a rabble of under-agers spills out. They prance about, bobbing and shouting and weaving and touching, and head to the pub with their fake IDs. The girls are waved through. 'It's not fair,' says seventeen-year-old Kevin.

'If you don't like it, go home to Mum,' says the bouncer.

Later one girl will lose her virginity, Kevin will vomit his dinner into the sand, and two other boys will 'cool off' in police cells until their parents come to pick them up and tell them off before tomorrow's picnic with Aunt Sheryl.

In the pub four friends finish a round. The fattest picks up his mobile phone and wipes some beer from it on to his once-white singlet. He dials a number and leans back in his chair, putting an arm up behind his head, exposing a wiry thatch of black hair against white fatty skin. 'Hello, Mum,' he says, then pauses. 'Hello, hello, can you hear me? It's this stupid phone, hello, can you . . .' He looks at the face of the phone and punches a few buttons. 'Fuckin' thing's stupid,' he says before lighting a cigarette. He exhales a blue cloud of smoke and then: 'Fuckin' batteries.'

A drag queen pops in for a hamburger before heading to the city for his show. Two Italian tourists watch with amusement. A businessman goes to the newsagent to pick up a girlie magazine before home. The afternoon paper too, to see what's on telly. Nose-ringed punks buy ice creams at the Danish ice-cream shop. Hippies sell beads. An older couple – he in a dinner suit, she in a silver cocktail dress – march quickly along the beachfront. A woman runs screaming along the footpath shouting insults in a foreign language. It could be one of many. Two lovers are fighting. Later, at home, their love-making will dry their tears.

For today at least.

# The Dust of My Passage
## GARRY P. SOMMERVILLE

FUNNY, THE SEEMINGLY random chain of events that will spark memories of another person. With no hint of its direction, suddenly you become aware that your subconscious has led you into an ambush with frighteningly tangible reminders of past ghosts. What is this perverse portion of our brains that forces us to retrace our steps down some previously visited avenue?

Yesterday, for instance. I'd been for a surf at Shipwreck and afterwards took the back road home. The hot air shimmered over the unsealed road beside Ninety Mile Beach and the dust of my passage hung curtain-like behind me. The distant Mangamukas twisted in the thermals and far-off windscreens winked from the Awanui straight.

I love driving like that, detached from physical action, floating above the Holden. The yellow lupin blurs and the cicadas scream a soundtrack. I could cruise for hours, but usually my speed creeps up until I start fishtailing on the corners and I bump back behind the wheel with a start.

This time though it was different. I rounded a bend and there were the turkeys in the middle of a small bridge. I could have stopped, but I saw roast drumsticks and a freezer full of replacements, so I gunned it. Six cylinders sang their song and the car leapt forward like a wolf on the fold. The birds moved slowly. The bridge sides prevented them leaping off and before the command to run had reached their succulent legs, I was amongst them.

Seven corpses and serious guilt. An ominous hissing as I stashed the last in the boot. I was still inspecting the damage, still drawing feathers from the radiator when I heard the approaching vehicle.

A farmer's tatty Land Rover. Farmers with old-fashioned ideas about property. My own flee command descended my spineless back and I bolted with my spoils.

I could see a waving arm, but I slowly opened out a lead as we flew along. Each corner now was a slide and correction, but I couldn't lose that Land Rover. Steam billowed over my windscreen, mixing with the dust into a mud smear. Only by pumping the washer, wipers on full, could I successfully negotiate the road.

The temperature gauge climbed steadily and the car stuttered. As it slowly died, I realised that my goose was cooked. And probably my motor. Reluctantly I pulled over to take it manfully.

'What's your hurry?' called my mate, Donut. 'Didn't you see me signalling? What's wrong with your car?'

'Shit. I thought you were the farmer.' Guilt had clouded my judgement and camouflaged his vehicle. 'Look,' I said, and with a theatrical gesture flung open the boot.

Seven stunned but grateful turkeys bolted, while I stood there and gaped at their flight.

I thought of you then. Reminded somehow of my surprise at your departure, of my anticipation and loss as my birds ran for the bush, leaving me hungry and confused while a busted radiator hissed its requiem.

# *Acceptance*
## MARGARET BRUENS

MA TEPANIA DIED on the first of May. I read it in the Death
Notices of the *New Zealand Herald*. She was 92 years old; I never knew
her Christian name was Gladys.

It's thirteen years since we left the farm. Ma and her family lived
further up the valley. Every fortnight, with her daughter Rose at
the wheel of the old yellow Buick, she would ride to town to collect
her pension.

In summer the car would race along the road leaving a cloud of
dust like a vapour trail, scattering the sparrows cavorting in their
dust baths.

When it rained, the Buick would shudder over the corrugated
road and up the hill, wheels spinning on the greasy surface. Once
released, it would bounce over the top and disappear from sight.

I first met Ma in town at the Waldorf Milkbar. I was sitting with
Ada, her niece, when I heard a penetrating voice. 'Bloody oath, Ada,
you look pale, you've been living too long with that Pakeha
husband.' She said something in Maori, and I heard the word
'Pakeha' mentioned again.

'You shouldn't swear so much, Aunty!'

'I'd swear even if the Queen of bloody England was here.'

I watched her walk the length of the shop - she usually wore
black, and with her white hair and long greenstone earrings, Ma
Tepania was a handsome figure.

'Your aunt doesn't like me. What did she say?' I whispered.

'You just give her back as good as she gives you.'

'Ma, what have you been up to? Your husband just walked

past and it looks like he's put his back out.'

'Someone knows what you're like, Aunty.'

Ma looked at me and grinned.

New people had taken over the Waldorf; he was a Dutchman.

'What do you think of this new man? City people don't know our ways,' Ma said, eyeing the man.

Rose went to the counter to order an ice-cream.

'Rose has been a good daughter - she scrubs those kids of hers as if she's going to wash away some of their colour. When she was young a teacher sent her a letter home telling me that Rose should wash more often. Bloody oath, I was mad! I wrote back: 'Dear sir, My Rose she no flower, you teach and not smell her!'

While Ma had been talking, she'd been watching the Dutchman. She rose to her feet. The man spread his arms, resting the palms on the counter. Ma mirrored his stance. She asked for two loaves of bread, speaking in Maori.

Rose stood behind her mother and indicated slicing bread.

'White or brown, madam?' asked the man. Ma replied, again in Maori, and Rose tapped her cheek.

'Brown? Certainly, madam.'

Ma then wanted butter, and Rose pretended to spread butter. This was followed by cigarettes and matches. Ma stood quietly, observing the man.

Then she said, 'I bet you can't milk a bloody cow.'

'I can even ride a bloody horse!' he replied.

There was a short silence.

'You're a bloody marvel, you are!'

# The Topiary Enthusiast
## JAN ROOKE

THE FOG DEEPENED, descending over the sleepy village, muffling the country sounds of birds preparing to roost. The shadows lengthening in the garden added a sinister air to the topiary animals, cloaking them in mystery.

She stood listening for the gravel and the sound of his key in the door. The grandfather clock in the hall struck seven, making her start as she peered around the wine-coloured velvet drapes. The smell of pastry drifted in from the kitchen. A rich steak and kidney pie, his favourite, would spoil if he didn't get home soon. From across the fields the church clock repeated the hour, its chimes hollow and ghostly.

A car sloshed its way down the empty lane, making her hold her breath for a few seconds. It drove past. She gave a loud sigh and made her way to the tiny kitchen. After turning the oven down she prodded a potato. It fell apart.

Later, pouring herself a large sherry, she wandered round the dining room, half-heartedly laying the table. The darkness was gathering outside the large leaded window. Crossing the room, it seemed to her that the absurd bushes she hated so much hovered in the gloom outside like malevolent spirits. What was the point in clipping a hedge to look like a squirrel or a cockerel? With his job in London and the hours he spent driving backwards and forwards, he hardly had time for her as it was, without spending every free moment making those monstrosities that held their eerie court outside. She could feel them watching her, judging her.

Her resentment, simmering on a low heat all these years,

suddenly cooled to icy fear as she caught sight of his hedging shears waiting by the back door. The church clock struck eight. A solitary dog barked. She downed her sherry in a gulp, then, taking the bottle with her, walked back into the lounge. There was another newsflash on the television, a pile-up on the southbound carriage of the M3. Turning the volume down, she stood for a while with the light off and the curtains parted, noticing for the first time how busy the tiny country lane was. At each low engine purr and stab of headlights her heart quickened, only to slow again as the car drove past.

As the clock struck ten she drew the curtains and locked the front door. In the kitchen, the uneaten food thrown away, the dishes stacked for washing, she carefully cleaned a tiny drop of brake fluid from the shears before hiding them under the sink.

Taking the sherry upstairs with her, she was surprised at how calm she now felt. She opened her bedroom curtains for one last look. The fog had lifted and a clear, starry sky shone down on the police car turning into her drive.

# The Dead Past
## HELEN MULGAN

AS A CHILD I lived on a poor coastal farm near Otaki. The farm's boundaries ran into sandhills on one side, and there my brother and I often played.

The contours of the sand were redrawn after every storm. We enjoyed finding new ridges, new valleys and new wind patterns, but one day we found a skull – half exposed, ancient and discoloured.

We had often been told of the skirmishes fought by the chief Te Rauparaha over this land, before he withdrew to nearby Kapiti Island, so we immediately decided that this was the skull of one of his warriors. We felt like archaeologists unveiling the past.

'We'll take it home and keep it like a trophy on the mantelpiece,' my brother decided.

'Mum mightn't like it,' I objected. 'We'd better keep it a secret.'

Proud though he was of his find, Jim could see the sense of that, so we smuggled our relic home. 'We'll keep it in your wardrobe.'

That was all right by me, until it was dark and I was alone. I felt the skull watching me with ill will through the wardrobe walls. I sneaked into my brother's room and asked him if he could take it over. He did not want to do that, but agreed to hide it in the lupin outside when our parents were safely asleep.

Next day those lupin bushes were fraught with menace. I fancied that a battalion of Maori warriors was there in spirit, waiting to avenge the disturbance of their brother's remains. And there were endless days and nights to come.

I was the first to snap, but Jim wasn't slow to humour me. So we told our parents.

We weren't really surprised that they took a quite different view of the disposal of archaeological remains.

'It was once part of a human being and must be respected.' My mother was very firm.

My father fetched a shovel and led the way. My brother was allowed to follow, carrying the skull. The farm dog fell in behind him. I was last and I carried my kitten for comfort against the uneasy presence of the supernatural.

Our little procession wound its way over farmland and up to the top of a far hill. I can recall the scene across the gulf of sixty-odd years. My father cleared the fern and dug the grave. My brother laid the old brown skull to rest. Then we all stood to attention looking out to Kapiti and my father said the Lord's Prayer.

It was all he had to offer. Man or woman, whaler, settler, warrior or wahine, he meant it cover any one of them. For me it was enough. The spirit world had received its due.

# Sacrifice to the Volcano God
## WITI IHIMAERA

NOT LONG AGO I walked into a bar in this Polynesian city and saw a beautiful young Maori girl dancing with a white boy. In the background was a huge papier-mâché volcano which, every now and then, erupted dry ice and showered laser beams.

My thoughts went back to the South Sea island movies I had seen. Burt Lancaster was in *His Majesty's O'Keefe*, Gary Cooper was in *Return to Paradise*, Yvonne de Carlo was the half-caste Luana in *Hurricane Smith*, Esther Williams was an American Tahitian in *Pagan Love Song* and, down in New Zealand, we had a little number called *The Seekers*. In this one, Jack Hawkins and Glynis Johns fought the Maori, and Indonesian actress Laya Raki played a Maori princess and did a dance with no clothes on. Willie Boy and I went to see *The Seekers* three times. Most of the movies were of the kind in which the local girl falls in love with the white hero. It's a pattern as old as Fletcher Christian himself and comes out of all those fantasies that white men have, that brown-skinned babes just love those hairy blond chests.

Then I remembered *Bird of Paradise*, set in Hawaii, which was typical of the formula. Handsome white man Louis Jordan comes to the islands where he falls in love with beautiful Polynesian girl Debra Paget, who is loved by local Hawaiian boy Jeff Chandler. No Polynesian girl I ever knew looked like Debra Paget, which was another reason for my cousin Georgina to get all hysterical and for Nanny Miro to mutter about her dopiness. It was just as bad for us Polynesian guys who felt we could in no way match up to the usual handsome white stereotype that our girls were falling for.

In the movie, Debra Paget walks on hot coals and, for some reason I still can't fathom, sacrifices herself to the volcano god. Wouldn't you just know it, but the volcano accepts the sacrifice of her life, and her sad but sorrowing white lover is able to go on with his life and sail off over the horizon to the arms of, presumably, the white woman back at home.

All this came to me, watching the Maori girl scattering the light in a bar one night not long ago.

Surely the volcano god has had his fill by now.

# Maori Bread
## KELLY MOREY

LILLIAN TE PAA dipped a teacup into the flour bin. When it came to the surface a small amount of flour toppled over the edge of the cup and back into the depths of the bin. She dumped what remained into a yellow plastic cylinder that sat in a bowl on the formica bench. Lillian repeated this exercise three times. The lid came off a tin of Edmond's baking powder. A teaspoon that lay on the bench shone wetly in the afternoon sun. Lillian clicked her tongue disapprovingly and wiped the offending moisture away with the hem of her skirt before dipping it into the white powder. A pinch of salt later and the ingredients were ready to be sifted. Long brown fingers wrapped around the handle of the sifter. Lillian squeezed the handle slowly, content to watch the snow drifts of flour float down, peppering then obliterating the plastic bowl bottom. Once the base was covered she picked up the tempo of her sifting. She never grew tired of the sifter, the delight was brand-new every time she brought it down from the shelf.

The Taiwanese-made Swiss cuckoo clock wheezed asthmatically, the large hand reached the twelve and the doors were flung open. A small bird shot out of the cubby hole and hiccupped four times. Lillian sucked her false teeth. 'Better get a move on, girl, the mokos'll be home soon.' She looked out the kitchen window, half expecting to see her grandchildren streaming across the home paddock. Dirty, hot and tired, their voices still shrill with excitement as they shouted about the trials of the day. She loved her grandchildren best when the last of them went to sleep at the end of a long day.

A cup of milk was added to the flour. A stiff dough clung to the sides of the bowl. Too much milk, girl. More flour was added and the dough formed a soft ball. The frying pan ticked away quietly on the heat in readiness. An old fruit tin had been filled with hini. It had cooled hard and white, and smelt rich with cooking juices. Lillian dug a large lump out with a tablespoon and flicked it into the pan. The lard began skating around madly as the heat chased it. Seconds later it surrendered and melted away without further protest.

The dough was deftly shaped into triangles and placed in the bubbling fat. The heat turned it golden. The triangles were flipped over to fry before being placed on newspaper to drain. The grease was drunk up by the newsprint, the paper becoming translucent as piece after piece of rich golden Maori bread was piled up. Blowflies buzzed around, excited by the cooking smells. Those mokopuna of mine really love the Maori bread, she thought happily as she sat down at the kitchen table to wait for them to return to her.

# *Kaha*
## LINDA CHATTERTON

I FIRST CAME across Kaha down Huapai way.

He was a mean-looking bugger. Big and brawny with the most evil eyes you'd ever seen. He'd just been kicked out of the pub for picking on a cow cocky. I was heading back home and he wasn't going anywhere special, so he hitched a ride.

I don't remember inviting him to stay. He just did.

That was six years ago.

Life round the Kaipara seemed to suit Kaha, but the locals were wary of him. He was a bit of a stirrer, and if he took a dislike to you, the only chance you had was to run like hell. Many a time I had to break up a scrap and drag him home battered and bruised. Someone threatened to shoot him once. Said there was no room for his sort round here.

Kaha didn't give a stuff. Nothing fazed him.

He earned his keep by doing the saleyard run with me and helping round the farm. He liked living rough and didn't care much for the finer things in life. But, man, did he like seafood.

Oysters, pipis and eels, they were his favourites. Most days he'd head off through the mangroves and go eeling. He overdosed on them once and was violently ill. Threw up on the kitchen floor. I thought he'd never look at eels again. But not Kaha. Next day he was back into them as usual.

Winter nights by the fire he'd listen to my stories about growing up on the Kaipara. How we collected toheroas on Muriwai Beach and cooked them on hot tin. And gathered firewood from the mudflats and fruit from the wild fig trees. And how we spent hours watching the barges carting sand up the harbour and fishing boats coming in with their hauls.

He knew my life history. I don't even know where he came from.

Kaha was a strange one, but I liked having him around. He could be a mean so-and-so when he wanted to, but we got along fine.

It's not easy burying a mate like Kaha. Six years is a long time. I'll miss him.

They say a dog is a man's best friend. And they're right.

# *The Finance Minister*
## ARTHUR KING

HE WAS A vain little man. Not about his appearance, remarkable only for his flaming red hair and peachy cheeks, but about his knowledge of politics and economics and his influence on the country's welfare. He boasted that all important government decisions originated with him. He even claimed responsibility for the most unpopular ones, believing that in time the people would come to recognise the wisdom – his wisdom – that had given them birth.

Secretly he despised the Prime Minister. The man was no leader and had no political nous. He had got where he was today because the people loved him. Sad that knowledge and ability had to come second to popular appeal, but he was sure it would not always be so. His day would come. If no love, there would be honour and respect.

The Minister often used small planes when flying on government business. He liked the broad view from his seat alongside the pilot, and most of all he liked the endless publicity the practice brought him.

The Prime Minister asked him one day, didn't he think he was being careless of his responsibilities? But he didn't follow the question with an instruction, so here the Minister was, on a bright blue autumn day, setting out once more in his favourite Cessna, this time to open a big shopping centre on the other side of the mountains.

He was writing on an A4 pad on his knees.

'Working on some new banking legislation,' he remarked to the pilot. No, it was not difficult. He'd studied banking all his life. He knew more about it than anyone else in the country.

A small silence before the pilot asked him whether he had ever considered a career in banking. More money at the top, without the uncertainty of politics.

The Minister laughed. 'My dear chap, bankers are such unimaginative fellows. One-track minds, you know, with percentage signs strewn all along the way. No originality – they all do the same things at the same time. A boringly mundane sort of life, which politics is anything but. And though I say it myself, not boastingly mind you, but as a simple statement of fact, there are many tracks in my mind, each shaped by knowledge and ability – altogether, greater knowledge and ability, I guess, than there is in the rest of the Cabinet combined. One day, no doubt, that knowledge . . .'

Those were all the words on the voice recorder the searchers found on the mountainside.

At the funeral the Prime Minister 'ventured to say' the country had lost one of the 'most colourful' political figures in its history.

# Dissociation
## DENIS BAKER

THAT IS THE kitchen table. This is a gas bill. This is an eviction notice. This is a demand. That . . . wump! . . . was a cockroach but is now a smear on the photograph of the ex-boyfriend that lost its glass when it connected with the closing door five weeks ago. That is another bill. So is that. That is junk mail. That is the rubbish bin.

Those are university books full of Important Ideas, Knowledge, Wisdom and Very Intelligent Arguments. Those are beautiful new boots, still in their box. Those are magazines. That is lipstick. That is the telephone number of the man from the café. That is the rubbish bin again. This is being strong.

There is gin. There is tonic. There is ice. There is lemon. There is hope.

That is the bed. That is a skirt. Those are legs. That is a tattoo. That is the wrong name. They are knickers. There is the thing that might heal over soon if something isn't done about it. These are jeans. That is a jumper. That is long brown hair, freed at last.

That is the television set. That is Judy Bailey and Richard Long. That is *The Fresh Prince of Bel Air*. No. That is M\*A\*S\*H. That was a commercial.

Those are plain, old everyday shoes. Those are socks. That is a toe. These are wonderful, gorgeous, brand-spanking-new boots, walking, jumping, kicking, pulverising. That is what these boots will do if they ever see them together. Anywhere. Ever. That was a full glass, wasted on the floor. This is being calm.

This is a full glass.

This is the telephone that does not ring.

That is the voice of the pizza man. That is a moan about rubber cheques. That is a promise and a lie. This is a gin.

This is a magazine with women who look like that, articles explaining how to look like that and articles explaining new ways to masturbate for those that don't look like that — and can't. This is a gin.

That is a half-empty pizza box. That is half a Michelangelo Supreme with extra spinach and no anchovies. Those are jeans with the top button undone. That is stomach.

Those are university books demanding attention. That is the television set. That is *Holmes*. That is a gin. That is *Shortland Street*. That is a big gin.

That is a party of five.

That is *X Files*.

That is something else.

This is the rubbish bin. That is the number of the man from the café — just in case.

That is an empty packet of potato chips. That was the Very Bad Late Movie. Those were the Valium the doctor prescribed. That is the end of the gin, the night, the hope, the strength. There is the telephone.

This is the telephone.

That is her voice denying he's there.

Those are my screams.

That is the dial tone.

These are my tears.

# Trains and Things
## KERRY DALTON

SHE TAKES OFF her motorcycle helmet and flicks back her hair. There is a mark across her nose where the helmet has been pressing. I notice new lines around her eyes, laughter lines. She grins at me and, without thinking, I grin back. Something turns over in my stomach.

'Long time no see,' she says.

'Mmmm,' I reply. Already I feel like I have given too much away.

She wanders up to the old steam engine and raps it with her knuckles. There is a booming sound. The noise echoes for a while, then stops. She is satisfied. It is a fanfare of sorts.

'Remember me working in that garden centre where they had that funny toy train that went around and around all day? The sound used to drive me crazy.'

I know what she is doing, casting for loops, seeing if they are still there. I get on with fixing the engine.

'Served a purpose though, it's how I got to meet you.'

And Ralph, I think. I want to tell her to stop, to go away, but pain overwhelms me. It is always like this. I get struck down in her presence. It's like the open road for her then, she can go where she likes.

'Where's Ralph then?' I manage to get out. I have revealed my rawness, but I have also knocked her off her stride.

'Let's just say we had a parting of the ways.'

I notice for the first time creases running from her nose to her mouth, puckers on her forehead. Maybe it hasn't all been good. Then she smiles and I hate her. I am back at the chess game, paralysed, watching them smile at each other.

They are an even match. Usually Francie wins hands down, but this time there is no telling which way the game will go. Ralph has just come off an oil rig. He says playing chess was just about all he did besides working – oh, and watching blue movies of course.

He looks at Francie when he says this. She looks back, straight into his eyes and smiles.

My brother, the games he still plays.

Finally I can't stand it any more and stand up, saying that I am going to bed. 'Don't be too long,' I say to Francie. She looks at Ralph and smiles, almost laughs.

Later I hear her bike start up and I feel like I am dying. I stay awake all night, waiting for her to come back. By morning I am numb. When I come into the empty lounge I notice that she won the game of chess.

That was a year ago. I had given up waiting for the motorbike's roar.

# The Talking Lily
## IAIN SHARP

I HEARD THE news on the radio while driving to work. Early this morning someone coshed the security guards and uprooted the celebrated 'Talking Lily of Kawhia'. Where the miraculous arum once lisped its controversial message, only a cavity remains. Aghast, botanists at the Institute of Environmental Science and Research have begged the thief, or thieves, to return the plant immediately.

They're whistling in the dark. The lily, I fear, is not just kidnapped but killed, and I believe its assassin(s) had the covert approval of the entire township of Kawhia.

Although they're not an unfriendly bunch, and although they could use the money, the five hundred or so inhabitants of Kawhia value their isolation too highly to encourage tourism. That's why the lily had to go. The commotion was wrecking the atmosphere.

The townsfolk don't mind an occasional day-tripper or two from Hamilton, but last month curious gawkers arrived in droves from all over the globe – Teutonic backpackers, Swedes in hired vans, busloads of amateur Japanese and Korean photographers. Moreover, every school in New Zealand organised a visit. A dozen times a day, children were commanded to sit in rows, hushed and miserable, while the lily addressed them.

Like most Aucklanders, Joy and I couldn't resist driving down for a peep and a listen. We joined a long queue in Kaoro Street one overcast Sunday afternoon. The fee of five dollars per head (babes-in-arms free of charge) was hardly extortionate, but the locals seemed ashamed of themselves as they collected the cash. They would rather have been out fishing.

There are many clusters of arum lilies on Kawhia's waterfront, but the talkative one stood alone, as if ostracised for its freakishness. Scientists were at a loss to explain the phenomenon, but if you bent down and applied an ear to the trumpet-like whorl of petals you could detect an indistinct whisper.

The narrator of Maurice Shadbolt's novel *Dove on the Waters* suggests that botany is boring because the only thing plants think about is sex. Following Shadbolt's lead, some listeners believed the lily's message was 'sexy'.

To my ear it sounded more like 'mercy'. Or perhaps the lily spoke in French ('merci'), or was commenting on the view ('mere sea').

Other interpretations included 'misty', 'messy', 'merrily', 'marshy' and even 'Marxist', but everyone agreed the lily was a limited conversationalist, content just to repeat a single remark ad infinitum. Frankly, after the initial surprise, Joy and I found the arum a bit of a bore – far less talented than the average cockatoo. For local entertainment, we preferred the ocean-sprayed sign on the wharf that announces to dull drivers: 'Highway 31 ends here'.

Immediately ahead of us in the queue was a twelve-year-old boy. We heard him whispering to the lily. 'Repeat after me, you stupid flower – piss and fuck and bollocks.'

'Mercy,' the lily replied. Or 'sexy'. Or 'measly'.

# Place of Work
## ROSEMARY TEARLE

IT ISN'T BAD as offices go. At least it gives the impression of being large and airy. As you come through the doorway you look straight out a large window – out to Princes Park two blocks away, down to rooftop gardens and retreats, and up to corporate logos on surrounding buildings. The window on the west wall can only offer buildings of aged shabbiness and run-down grunge, but each afternoon it apologises by handing you a streaming sun.

The window ledges are wide and call out to you to store files, phone books and foliage on them. The furniture is functional, conservative and adequate – not at all designed to keep manufacturers of such in business, just designed to allow you to do your job. The typewriter is manual. Manual! In this day and age! But all you use it for is to change a few addresses, write a letter from time to time when the secretary is away, and fill out the occasional form for a bureaucratic government department. So an electronic machine remains a dream in a world of practical reality.

The wall and ceiling decor, deliberately muted and discreet, whispers faintly above the aggressive roar of the carpet. It means to be noticed, this synthetic creature whose lot in life is to allow all and sundry to trample it underfoot. Squatting on the carpet, under the westward-looking window, is the permanent resident of the office. There it squats, day in, day out, huffing and puffing – sometimes heatedly, sometimes icily – to anyone who cares to listen to its attempts to keep the office an environmentally friendly place to be. Each facet of the office reflects the other work that is conducted in this room.

The carpet echoes the aggression that is enacted upon it each lunch hour; the icy reception to the heated passion that is huffed and puffed; the practical reality of a job, any job in this recession keeping her mute; hope is not found in the sightless eyes in the buildings opposite. Only the windows have something to offer: the solace of a view of far horizons, the peace of the cool green trees and the healing caress of the sun's rays as they tiptoe sympathetically over the window ledge at violation's end.

And what have you to offer? Outrage to strengthen and support? Speculation as to why? Relief because it isn't you? Disgust because she allows it to happen? Financial speculation as to the length of continuation? Agreement because the man who pays the piper calls the tune?

Violette – yes, she has a name for she is a person – goes to the toilets, where she purges her body of his slime and power and vomits her disquiet and misery into the toilet bowl.

# *It Rained in the Night*
## IDOYA MUNN

IT RAINED IN the night and the next day she went to school. Her teacher said now we have read six stories we have read six stories and then the teacher counted them aloud, reciting the titles the authors saying now we are enriched.

But she was writing a story – she was writing and nobody knew and the teacher said what do you think what do you think and the teacher didn't know, nobody knew that that morning she had walked past a dead cat a dead stiff cat wet stuck-together fur looked like it was lying normally until you turned it over and saw it was flat on one side and they'd stood there outside on an almost cold nearly winter morning in their dressing gowns looking at this flat on one side cat trying to work out if it was theirs, trying to remember what their cat looked like, it had rained in the night.

She ate two marshmallow easter eggs for morning tea and she smoothed out the shiny gold purple pink paper and the chickens the rabbits but no there weren't any dead cats flat on one side cats, no wet fur stuck-together cats that you weren't quite sure were yours or not.

It rained in the night, and she had been so happy that it was raining oh I love the rain she had said, it is getting so wonderfully winter and she hadn't known, had she, that the next morning, just when she was going to get the paper, she would walk past a dead cat.

Surely, she thought, surely you find the disasters of the day on the front page of the newspaper not just to the right of the driveway lying stiff wet flat on one side.

She felt sick from eating two marshmallow easter eggs for morning tea she looked at the shiny paper on the table – you didn't know before you ate the easter eggs that you would feel sick, but there is such pleasure to be had from eating two easter eggs one straight after the other even when you have finished one you know there is still one more to go.

The yellow batteries on the table beside her said warning do not dispose of in fire put in backwards may explode leak get hot causing personal injury.

What is personal injury, she thought, is it walking down to get the paper not knowing you would see a dead stiff flat on one side cat or is it eating marshmallow easter eggs straight after the other disposing in fire putting in backwards leaking exploding getting hot.

Or maybe it is smoothing out the shiny gold purple paper and ripping holes in the rabbits the chickens, but not dead stiff flat on one side cats they don't draw pictures of those on shiny gold purple pink marshmallow easter egg paper.

It rained in the night.

# *Breaking Up*
## JANETTE SINCLAIR

WHEN NOLAN ASKED Rosaline to leave she went to pieces, launching her favourite teapot at the window he was fixing. The cunning diamonds of leadlight stood firm, but the teapot smashed into pointed blue florets of Greek Valerian.

She drove all night round wild windy bays listening to talkback radio. Disembodied voices of insomnia, paranoia and megalomania jostled the dark air waves. A moon, axed and sickly, limped from ragged eastern hills to a skyline pierced by wind turbines and radar aerials, trailing fractionated light like drops of moonblood on the harbour.

Returning at the weekend to collect her belongings, she found Nolan had changed the locks and left two suitcases full of books and clothes (poetry and cookery, clean and soiled, all mixed up) on his newly trellised porch. She composed a letter requesting 'the repatriation of property I willingly contributed to our domestic arrangement, viz waterbed, kitchen whizz and CD player', but her pen hovered, momentarily indecisive, over 'Regards, Rosaline' versus 'R. Powell'.

The reply from Nolan's solicitor, outlining arrangements for 'the recovery of said effects, and appropriate compensation for loss of dwelling in the interim', was addressed to 'Ms Rosalin Powell'. What hurt more than those formal phrases denying the empathy of eight years was the missing syllable, that 'e' of élan, elegance, equilibrium.

She was two months in her new flat when she received an anonymous phone call late at night. 'Roslin . . . Yes, Roslin . . . Ohyes, OhyesohyesohyesRoslin . . .' But she'd got herself an unlisted number, and the only thing she could think of was that wretched computer at work. With the installation of a new payroll system, she had been irrevocably entered as Roslin Powell. She'd given up after three attempts to correct this, when each time funds got debited from her account and the bank manager finally decided to slash her overdraft in the light of her newly uncoupled status.

One weekend she found a part of herself in the Personal Column: 'Sensual sensitive 40+ professional woman . . .' Well why not, she decided after some thought. She wrote to several numbers and finally arranged to meet a mathematician who worked in Chaos Theory. For their first dinner together she wore a jersey silk dress in brilliant kaleidoscope squares and diamonds and talked intelligently of 'Arcadia' and *Jurassic Park*.

'That dress,' said the mathematician, as he eyed her laid out on the ivory counterpane of his bed. 'It's like Rubik's cube.'

'Play with my squares then,' she murmured, closing her eyes.

'The pattern needs rearranging, Ros . . . Ros, Ros . . . Let me solve the puzzle . . . let me get to the solution . . .'

She never saw the scissors swooping, black as leadlight crossbars.

# *Telesa*
# CHERIE BARFORD

TELESA IS A presence. She was a mortal who was taken by immortals and made eternal. She's found in Samoa, especially along the road to Aleisa.

That's where my grandfather saw her. He was inspecting a copra plantation when she appeared at the side of the road, sitting on a rock, combing her hair.

She has beautiful hair. It's as black as the lava that shines razor-sharp along Savai'i's coast.

Opa noticed that her body was oiled. It glistened in the heat. 'What do you want?' he asked.

Telesa smiled. Her mouth split open like a ripe mango, the skin peeling back from the flesh. 'Leave me alone!' he shouted as she walked towards him.

Then his horse bolted, running through the plantation, jumping piles of copra drying in the sun.

I have also seen Telesa. It was when my cousin lay dying in my grandmother's house. Siene was weak from fever. Her lips were cracked. Her eyes closed.

It was Sunday and the family was together for the day. The men were outside preparing the umu. The women sat around Siene. Children ran in and out of the house.

'What shall we do?' I asked my grandmother. 'We've prayed, fasted, chanted, sung hymns, massaged Siene and given her medicine from the hospital.'

'What will be will be,' Oma replied. She sat with Siene's head on her lap, stroking the matted curls covering her knees. 'She has such beautiful hair,' said Oma.

Outside, the men laughed as they covered the umu. They'd wrapped the chickens, taro and bananas in tinfoil instead of taro leaves. We could hear them exclaiming at the silver parcels.

'What a palagi umu!' said Tavita.

'A real Kiwi job,' Sione agreed. 'Next thing, we'll be using newspaper instead of leaves to cover it!'

The women laughed. Some of them had seen the family in New Zealand make an umu without any leaves at all!

We were still laughing when Telesa appeared. It was frightening. She looked so angry. Everyone stood still. The children whimpered and clung to their mothers.

'Well,' said Oma, smiling at Telesa, 'I know what you want.'

She leaned over Siene, reached into her handbag and drew out a cloth parcel. It unrolled to reveal her barber's scissors. They were shiny and sharp. One of her prized possessions.

'Telesa,' she scolded, snipping Siene's hair. Short, metallic snips around the fevered crown. 'You have your own beauty. Don't envy this poor girl.'

'Here.' She held up an armful of black waves. 'Take this. Leave the girl alone!'

Telesa nodded. Took the hair. Disappeared.

Then Siene opened her eyes and smiled.

# *Almost a Perfect Day*
## BILL GRUAR

SUNSHINE SLANTED ONTO the beach, dancing in the lines of small waves rippling away on both sides as sea quietly met sand.

She removed her sunglasses, closed one eye and squinted out to sea through a small telescope. Two specks became apparent. Were they still swimming out to sea? Had one given up so they could return? Too far out to tell. She sighed, replaced the sunglasses, rolled over and continued sunbathing. It all seemed so silly, so pointless.

Another foolish competition. As if she cared. How arrogant to assume that one day she would choose between them and that would be that. Never really talking to her about it at all. Taken for granted, a trophy in a mindless competitive game.

Competitions. The wet towel draping should have been the last straw. Why couldn't they see that she wasn't impressed? What had she done to encourage this? The three of them would have to stop meeting together.

And who would be the judge this time? A race on the sand or timing a drinking session were entirely different. It would have to be a gentleman's agreement. Men are such fools, she thought, slapping at a sandfly on her thigh, noting with distaste the quiver of tissue. Perhaps she would have to make up her mind sometime . . .

They were certainly a long way out, she noted through the telescope. Were there still two heads, or had they merged into one larger, if less distinct blob? She couldn't tell. A cloud moved across the sun and she drew up her knees. A bit late in the year for sunbathing, the season's almost gone, she thought.

Ah, there's a head. A bit closer in, is it? Now, where's the other one? She looked further out but could see nothing. An arm appeared briefly above the head in front of her, and disappeared. Then the head disappeared too.

She looked in angry disbelief through the inadequate instrument. Where'd he go? Christ! Getting to her feet, she ran to the water. Jim, or Frank or whoever you are, stop fooling about . . .

But the glass showed nothing: an empty ocean, an empty horizon. She turned for someone to confirm her fears, but the beach too was empty, as she well knew.

She gave them five minutes, chewing one nail to the quick, then dropped the telescope on the sand, ran for the nearest phone.

# *Acquainting the M'Col Col*
# BERNARD BROWN

COMMUNICATION RECEIVED FROM *Father Stampl, Central New Britain Catholic Mission 1931–1950 (dated July 1953):*

'Hisiu, whose account essentially this is, up to the time of the visitation of 'The Stranger', was an unremarkable villager. Like some of his fellows he openly disparaged the Kapitan (the local Australian official): otherwise he showed no interest in local affairs which, by 1937, had unaccountably deteriorated.

'Yet, upon 'The Incident' (described below) Hisiu took charge and remained – even through the Japanese occupation – in total control of village life. After resumption of the Australian mandate in 1948, he was convicted under the Native Regulations for Spreading False Reports, and gaoled. Before completing his sentence he was transferred to Mosman, New South Wales, to attend a trade union leadership course. He contracted an illness there in 1949 and died in Sydney.'

It was a matter calling for involvement of a stranger. Kin wouldn't do, even kin drawn from the other villages, for blood and marriage make a cockroach of neutrality. Plainly we had to disregard the one known as the *Kapitan*, whose talk, out of a book, is not the fashion of our tongue and nothing like our Father's way – a sharper, suppler equity.

Prayers had been tried, and sorcery. But still a shell-edge sullenness prevailed, pointing in my view to weakening of ties and *wantok* discipline.

Then came the hairless one. Darker than us (though some thought not so dark), old-young, set taut and straight, yet frail; an unenlisted wisdom in his eyes – or was it vacancy? Even the women's talk was stilled. The dogs sloped off to hide.

Confronting us without the sign of doubt or fear, he took an axe from where it lay and, in one movement, bent, cut off a toe and held it up for all to see.

There was no blood. Was there no sanity?

A spear thumped in his breast. A rain of spears. We fell upon him, digging, hacking with our blades. All screaming curses, bile and rage. Eructing death, exalting.

Just as suddenly, as one, we stopped. For seconds stood transfixed – then numb, like wooden things, backed off the mashed, contorted prey.

There was no blood. That was and is the mystery.

There is no need, I think, of gods or *Kapitans*, of books or mediator kin (and least of all of sorcery). For now there are no feuds, no trespassing of pigs, few thefts and seldom an adultery. Occasional disputes, when they occur, are brought straight away to me. For now the people know I keep the peace, enforce the harmony. I own the power. I am the law. For all the people know I wear about my neck the bloodless stranger's toe.

# *End Game*
## GORDON STEVENS

JOHN'S FADED RED Escort jounced down the shingled clay drive. His two-tooth ewes grazed unflustered in the lush grass. They were looking good. The grass was holding longer this year with such a wet spring. Indeed, his lawns were as high as the rain gauge. Must get them cut before Christmas.

Since Mum left and he'd graded the front fence out it was a simple ten minutes of tight driving on the tractor with the hay mower and they were done.

His slim frame looked neat in the new dark suit. Now he was regional chairman for the electorate, he needed it, though the extra cost of replacing the worn cowboy boots annoyed him. There was another fifteen years' wear in them.

Groceries were easy from long habit. Fishfingers, frozen stir-fry veges for boiling, tomato sauce, bread and ice-cream.

He called into Farmrite and lifted two plastic containers of drench into the boot. The little car settled and loose tennis balls rolled around the back ledge.

The usual people were at the meeting, the usual concerns. Super surtax, beef prices, how the DPB had destroyed the fabric of society, albeit already seriously frayed by marijuana and indiscriminate couplings.

It was late for someone to be on the roadside. And a bit off the usual hitch-hiking tracks.

She smiled.

He saw freckles, red hair and the Canadian maple leaf on the tiny red pack.

'Hi, I'm Angie. I've been working on the skifield.'

With heart-beating painful politeness he suggested that she spend the night at his farmhouse.

After supper he listened to her talk. The silent TV in the corner of the bare lounge. Outside the lush green, the cheeping fledglings, the sheep coughing settled into night.

Later he lay and watched her snuggled on his arm, trusting, quiet in her sleep.

Angie began working in a farm accountant's office in town. He bought a small white diesel station wagon for her to use.

Every day Angie would bring home something else. Bunches of dried flowers, framed posters, red enamel pots.

He would come in for lunch, wash the sheep off his hands and wander in the cool of the lounge, picking up, for the sheer joy of holding them in his hands, the smooth soapstone carvings that she bought at Trade Aid.

Together they would go to the weekend craft fairs and browse amongst the blue glassware.

They often sat silent in the evenings as the glow of the sunset lit up the comfortable friendly knick-knacks in their niches and shelves around the lounge.

It was a year exactly. She took only her red pack.

He gave the white station wagon to a niece at university. She picked it up from the airport carpark.

He has people back for a whisky after tennis these days.

And sits relaxed as he discusses the price of cattle.

His eyes move around the familiar room.

He says, 'I hold her in my heart, and sometimes it's like she's not really gone.'

# *Justice Denied*
## CHRIS McVEIGH

MR JUSTICE ALAN France did not suffer fools gladly. Wise men didn't get off much better. In fact, given the power he wielded, the whole human race came in for a bit of a battering. He was a man (no, not just a man – one of Her Majesty's Judges) for whom the word 'impartial' meant being equally unpleasant to both sides.

Now he was on circuit. Not that they'd tell him this, but the Christchurch Bar and Bench were experiencing one of their rare forensic breathers while he flung his weight about in Auckland.

It had been a long Friday: two interim injunctions, a tedious family protection case involving the usual splenetic outpourings of greedy siblings, and now – a sentencing. Normally these were dealt with first thing in the morning, but this one was different. Some silly woman had pleaded guilty that afternoon to a drugs charge. Why women had become lawyers, let alone involved in illegal commercial activities, was beyond him. When he was a boy, women did what nature had suited them to. Looked after men. Mothers, wives, sisters – they were all there to minister to the needs of the people who really ran the planet.

He shifted in his chair.

The earnest and, regrettably, bearded young man who was appearing for this hapless harpy was doing his best: '. . . deprived background . . . drug habit . . . solo mother . . .'

Oh dear, what a pity. Should I send her a food parcel? On a free trip to Waikiki perhaps?

Four years' imprisonment. He savoured the resonance of his own words as the stunned family of the teenage delinquent clasped one another in futile grief.

He rose to leave. As the registrar intoned the standard litany of departure his eye was caught by a shaking fist. Presumably the father of the adolescent felon. Strange the way his beard almost hid a crescent-shaped birthmark on his cheek. Play by the rules, that's what the judge had been taught. And it worked. Not just worked, was right.

In his chambers, he thought about the Bar dinner that night. Welcoming the new Silks to the Auckland Bar. A glossy affair with a number of Court of Appeal judges to burnish the edges. He folded the last tuck into his silk bow tie.

Later he strolled out into Princes Street. What a wonderful evening. Champenoise, brilliant speeches, satisfactory food (although the roast beef of his youth had been given unnecessary continental élan by the addition of red wine and bone-marrow sauce. Whatever had happened to gravy?)

He slipped the security card through the slot. The door of the club where he was staying sprang open.

In his elegant room he changed into his new plum-red pyjamas. His wife slumbered and, so as not to wake her, he went out to use the corridor toilet.

The door was stuck. He pushed hard. It fell open. A stairwell beckoned, a concrete stairwell. The door had closed. It couldn't, wouldn't open. He was in the bowels of the wretched building. How was he going to get back? He looked up. A flight of concrete steps, at the top, a door.

Freedom.

Pulling it open in cold anxiety, he barely noticed the chill of the air. It clicked shut at the same moment as he saw the 2 a.m. traffic of Shortland Street racing by.

Some hours later, having hidden behind an obliging marble pillar, he realised what his only alternative was. It was raining. The club was impregnable. His pyjamas were imperfect as outdoor raiments. He was very cold. Not just cold . . . freezing.

A cab cruised up from Jean Batten Place. He leapt out, arms waving. The cab lurched to a halt, the back door opened. All vestiges of judicial dignity gone, he flung himself in, slammed the door shut.

The first thing he noticed was the maternal warmth of the sheepskin seat covers.

The second was the crescent-shaped birthmark almost hidden by the driver's beard.

# Notes on Contributors

**P. A. Armstrong** was born in 1934 in Putaruru. After two years of secondary education he worked as a plumber for a small building firm, then as a process worker at the Kinleith timber mill. Now retired and with his four children having left home, he is able to indulge his lifelong pleasure in reading, and has recently begun to write.

**Denis Baker** was born in Auckland in 1966 and has an MSc. His writing has been broadcast on National Radio. He lives in Kingsland, Auckland, not New York City, and is currently dogless. He spends 'his holidays in regression and nights in terror'.

**Cherie Barford** was born in 1960 to a German-Samoan mother and a Palagi father, and grew up in West Auckland. The mother of two sons, she works as a performance poet and teacher. She has published two collections of poetry and her writing has appeared in numerous magazines and anthologies, including *New Women's Fiction 4* (New Women's Press, 1991).

**Rhonda Bartle** was born in New Plymouth in 1954 and grew up in Taranaki 'somewhere between Elvis and the Beatles'. Her writing has been published in the *Listener* and *Metro*. Her first child was born in 1972 and her fifth in 1993. She is currently studying journalism through the Open Polytechnic.

**Maggie Bartlett** was born in Australia in 1943 and at the age of forty completed her BA in literature, music and education. She now lectures trainee teachers in music in Dunedin and studies Buddhism and the Tibetan language. Her short stories for children and adults have been broadcast and published in New Zealand and Canada.

**Kath Beattie** was born in the Coromandel in 1937. She was a boarder at Epsom Girls' Grammar, then trained as a teacher before teaching in New Zealand and overseas. Currently a social worker, she also writes for adult and children's publications. She has a love of the outdoors and cryptic crosswords.

**Norman Bilbrough** was born in Feilding in 1941. He has published numerous stories and two works of fiction, *Man With Two Arms* (1991) and *The Birdman Hunts Alone* (1994). He lives in Wellington, where he works as a fiction assessor, writer and teacher of creative writing.

**Tamzin Blair** was born in New Plymouth in 1976. She is currently completing Owen Marshall's fiction writing course in Timaru. She has had several works published in literary magazines and has completed a collection of short stories that she is expecting to have published late in 1997.

**Richard Brooke** was born in Christchurch in 1948 and educated there and in Sydney. He has travelled extensively and worked in Asia. He has published a number of stories and articles in New Zealand and overseas and is currently Head of English at Green Bay High School in Auckland.

**Bernard Brown** was born in England in 1934. He has taught law in Singapore and New Guinea and at the University of Auckland, where he is an associate professor. His writing has been chiefly in the area of legal regulation, but he has also published three collections of poetry, including *Surprising the Slug* (Cape Catley, 1996).

**Diane Brown** was raised in Auckland and lives there still. She tutors ESL, creative writing and is a book reviewer. Her first book, *Before the Divorce We Go to Disneyland* (Tandem Press, 1997), is a narrative blend of poetry and prose. In her small amounts of free time she enjoys scrambling around rocks and boogie boarding.

**Margaret Bruens** was born in New Plymouth. After working as a cadet on the *Taranaki Herald* she took creative writing courses at Victoria University of Wellington and at the London Media Workshop. She has also been involved with drama, both acting and writing. She now lives in Titirangi, Auckland, and does freelance writing.

**Linda Chatterton** was born in Christchurch in 1949 and educated at Linwood High School. Her fiction has been published in women's magazines in New Zealand and Australia. She lives at Titahi Bay and is employed as a sales representative for a hosiery company. An avid cricket fan, she also enjoys craft work.

**Frances Cherry** was born in Wellington in 1937 to Communist parents. She has no educational qualifications, having married young and mothered five children. She was divorced at forty and 'life began'. She has had numerous short stories and two novels published. She loves walking in the early morning on Paekakariki Beach.

**John Connor** was born in Lancashire in 1947 and has lived in New Zealand since 1966. He was co-winner of the Reed Fiction Award in 1989 with his short story collection *Distortions*, and his stories were anthologised in *Tart and Juicy* (1994) and *Lust* (1995). He is employed as a lecturer at the Manukau Institute of Technology.

**Kerry Dalton** was born in 1963 and grew up in Auckland. She graduated from Victoria University of Wellington in 1986 with First class Honours in History and English Literature. She currently lives in Wellington and is the mother of a young daughter. 'Trains and Things' is her first published work.

**Waiata Dawn Davies** was born in Levin in 1925 and educated in Hastings, at Ardmore Teachers' College and the University of Queensland. The mother of eight sons, she taught for forty-two years, mostly in Rotorua. She has published two collections of poetry and her short stories have won awards. Her other interests are music and gardening.

**Patricia Donnelly** was born in Stockport, England, in 1936 and educated in Manchester and Loughborough. She trained as a librarian before emigrating to New Zealand in 1963. She is now a full-time writer of prose and poetry. Her first novel, *Feel the Force*, was published by the Collins Crime Club in 1993.

**Marie Duncan** was born in Wellington in 1949. She has a history degree from Victoria University and works as an administrator for an accountancy practice. She writes in the weekends and two of her stories have been broadcast on radio.

**Lauris Edmond** grew up in Hawke's Bay and today lives in Wellington. Best known for her twelve volumes of poetry, she has also written plays, prose fiction and a three-volume autobiography. She travels widely at home and abroad and has an honorary doctorate in literature from Massey University.

215

**Peter Edmonds** was born in England in 1919. Educated at Imperial College, Windsor, he served around the world in the Royal Engineers from 1939 until 1958. He emigrated to New Zealand in 1974 and worked as a civil engineer until he retired in 1984. His interests are reading, especially history, and writing.

**Chris Else** was born in England in 1942 and educated at Auckland Grammar and the University of Auckland. He has been a postman, storeman, teacher, lecturer, bookseller, computer programmer, consultant and literary agent. His books include *Why Things Fall* (Tandem Press, 1991) and *Endangered Species* (Hazard Press, 1997).

**Jan Farr** was born in Hokitika in 1940. After being first published in 1966, she has written radio and stage plays, children's books and stories. In 1996 she graduated from Bill Manhire's writing course at Victoria University of Wellington. She has two adult children and lives in Owhiro Bay, Wellington.

**Fiona Farrell** was born in Oamaru in 1947. Educated at Otago and Toronto Universities, she has an MPhil in Drama. She has two daughters and lives on Banks Peninsula, where she writes and gardens. Her most recent book is *Six Clever Girls Who Became Famous Women* (Penguin, 1996).

**Victoria Feltham** was born in Dunedin in 1949. She has a BA (Hons) in Philosophy. Her stories have been broadcast and published in the literary magazines *Sport* and *Takahe*. Married with four children, she now lives in Wellington, where she is doing an MA in Creative Writing at Victoria University.

**Graeme Foster** was born in Te Awamutu in 1944 and educated at local schools and the University of Auckland, where he graduated

BA. He has published five books, which include poetry, short stories and recreational walks. He is a gardener interested in the conservation of native forests.

**Sarah Gaitanos** was born in London in 1950, raised in rural Wairarapa and educated at boarding school in Hawke's Bay. She has a BA from the University of Canterbury and has published three short books of children's fiction. She lives in Lower Hutt with her Greek husband, three teenage sons and female animals. She also sings in the Orpheus Choir.

**Patricia Grace** was born in Wellington in 1937, of Ngati Raukawa, Ngati Toa and Te Ati Awa descent. She is the author of seven works of adult fiction – short stories and novels – and three children's books, several of which have won awards. Her first book was *Waiariki* (1975); her most recent, *The Sky People* (1994). She lives in Plimmerton.

**A. K. Grant** was born in Wanganui but has lived most of his life in Christchurch. A lawyer by profession, he ended up drifting between the hard bright lights of that world and the shadowed regions of TV scriptwriting and humorous journalism. He lives in Christchurch with a rare collection of his own works.

**Barbara Grigor** was born in post-war Germany of Polish parents and came to New Zealand at the age of two. She lives in Auckland, is a registered nurse and is married with four children. She is currently working on a novel as well as studying English at Massey University.

**Bill Gruar** was born in Hamilton in 1947 and educated in Christchurch. He edited *Canta, Focus* and the *New Zealand Whole Earth*

*Catalogues*, toured with Blerta, worked in film-making, played in bands, farmed and made furniture. The father of five, he lives in Waterview, Auckland. An accident in 1995 made him a paraplegic, a story he tells in *Spinal Dogs* (Valid Press, 1996).

**Roger Hall** was born in Essex, England, in 1939. He has been a teacher, watersider, waiter, car-assembly worker, editor and parent. He writes plays, pantomimes and musicals for the stage, radio and television. His other interests are reading, tennis, golf, walking, travel and watching television.

**Jenni-Lynne Harris** was born in Wellington in 1959. A BA (Hons) graduate from Victoria University, she is also a trained teacher in English and German. Married with four children, she has recently started writing and has published three children's books. She is also interested in sport, reading and crafts.

**Tim Higham** was born in England in 1962 and grew up in Eltham, Taranaki. Today he lives in Christchurch, where he works as a publicist for Antarctica New Zealand. He writes regularly on natural history and has won journalism awards for his work. Married with two daughters, he enjoys food, wine, literature and snorkelling for seafood.

**Pauline Humphries** was born in wartime Britain and has lived in New Zealand for thirty years. She has one son and has worked at nearly everything. She lives in Wellington and runs technical writing workshops and studies literature extramurally through Massey University. She is currently working on a novel.

**Witi Ihimaera** was born in Gisborne in 1944. He is the author of ten books of fiction. His first was *Pounamu Pounamu* (1972), the first book of short stories to be published by a Maori writer. His novel *Bulibasha* (1994) won the Montana Book Award. Since 1992 he has been editing a five-volume anthology of Maori writing, *Te Ao Marama*.

**Kevin Ireland** was born in Auckland in 1933. He lives in Devonport, on Auckland's North Shore. The author of twelve works of poetry, his latest books are the poems, *Skinning a Fish* (Hazard Press, 1995), a short story collection, *Sleeping with the Angels* (Penguin, 1995), and the novel *Blowing My Top* (Penguin, 1996).

**Arthur King** was born in Christchurch in 1913. Educated at Christchurch Boys' High, he then worked in journalism in Christchurch and London. During the Second World War he wrote for Army Education's current affairs publications and later joined an advertising agency. He now writes, reads and gardens enthusiastically at Paraparaumu Beach.

**Rachael King** was born in Hamilton in 1970 and grew up in Auckland. She recently completed a BA in English at the University of Auckland, which included Albert Wendt and Witi Ihimaera's creative writing paper. A former bass player and radio announcer for bFM, she is Books Editor and ad rep for *Pavement* magazine.

**Graeme Lay** was born in Foxton in 1944. He grew up in Taranaki and graduated from Victoria University of Wellington in 1967. He has published short stories, novels and works of non-fiction. He lives in Devonport, on Auckland's North Shore, and enjoys reading, swimming, walking and travel. He is Books Editor of *North & South* magazine.

**Ross Lay** was born in Wellington in 1963 and educated at Green Bay High, Auckland, the United World College, Singapore, and the

University of Auckland, where he graduated BA in English and Politics. He currently lives in central Auckland and is a parent, teacher and gardener. He has published several poems and short stories.

**Sue McCauley** was born in the Wairarapa in 1941. She attended Nelson Girls' College, then worked as a copywriter and journalist before publishing her first novel, *Other Halves* (1982). She has two adult children and now lives in Christchurch with her second husband. Her latest novel is *A Fancy Man* (Vintage, 1996).

**Joy MacKenzie** was born in Hamilton in 1947. She has three sons and an MA (Hons) from the University of Auckland. A poet, fiction writer and ESL teacher, she won the *Sunday Star* short story contest in 1991 and received the Lilian Ida Smith Award in 1994. Her poems and stories have been published in literary magazines and broadcast on radio.

**Chris McVeigh**, QC, was born in Christchurch in 1945 and educated at Christ's College and the University of Canterbury. He was a member of the original cast and a scriptwriter for the TV programme *A Week of It*. The father of four daughters, he has recently co-authored *Second Wind*, a book about middle-age separation.

**Owen Marshall** was born in Te Kuiti in 1941. Educated in Blenheim, Timaru and Christchurch, he has an MA (Hons) from the University of Canterbury. A former teacher and now a full-time writer in Timaru, he is the author of eight short story collections and a novel, has been the recipient of numerous fellowships and was Katherine Mansfield Memorial Fellow in 1996.

**Valerie Matuku** was born in Hawera in 1946 and was educated there until she went to training college. She has been a teacher all her life, currently in Wanganui. Her stories have been published in magazines and broadcast on radio. In 1996 she was the winner of the Ripping Good Read competition.

**Rowan Metcalfe** was born and raised in the rural heartlands of New Zealand. She left for Europe in 1975 and spent seventeen years in England, where she was involved in community work, had two children and edited a quarterly journal. She now travels between Europe and the Pacific, researching a semi-fictional biographical novel.

**Thomas Mitchell** was born in Auckland in 1971. He has tertiary qualifications in English, Spanish, speech and drama, and currently works as a librarian. Some of his poetry has appeared in the Internet journal, *Trout*. He goes to church, the opera and 'for long Borgesian strolls'.

**Kelly Morey** was born in 1969 in Kaitaia and grew up in Papua New Guinea. Now living in the Far North, she has worked as a waitress, veterinary nurse and lawn mower. In 1997 she will complete her BA and finish writing her first collection of short stories. 'Maori Bread' is her first published work.

**Michael Morrissey** was born in Auckland in 1942. He has published nine books of poetry and over eighty short stories. His work *The Fat Lady & The Astronomer* won the PEN Best First Book of Prose award in 1982. His latest book, *Paradise to Come* (1997), consisting of two novellas, is published by HarperCollins.

**Martha Morseth** was born in the United States in 1938 and educated at Minnesota and Pennsylvania Universities. She has lived in Dunedin since 1972, and is Head of English at St Hilda's

Collegiate School. Her writing has been published in a variety of New Zealand magazines and literary journals.

**Helen Mulgan** was born in Hamilton during the Great Depression. She was educated in Wanganui and graduated from Victoria University of Wellington and Library School. She worked as a librarian before and after raising a family at York Bay, Eastbourne. Her interests are reading, bush walking, Amnesty New Zealand and New Zealand art.

**Idoya Munn** was born in Madrid in 1974 and grew up in various suburban Auckland areas. She was educated at Auckland Girls' Grammar and the University of Auckland, graduating BA in Spanish. In 1990 she won the Wattie Goodman Fielder Young Writer of the Year Award. She works in Auckland, in a TV post-production house.

**Patricia Murphy** was born in Manchester and now lives in the Hutt Valley. She has worked as a lampshade maker, statistics gatherer and speechwriter. She graduated BA from Victoria University of Wellington in 1984. Her short stories and poems have been published in magazines and broadcast on radio.

**Rose Omar** was born in Timaru. She has lived most of her life in Christchurch and is a registered nurse. Married with two young children, she has been studying creative writing at Hagley Community College for the last year. She is interested in fiction writing, travel and Asian cooking.

**Jonathan Owen** was born in London in 1944 and educated in England. He has lived for a number of years in France and has been a resident of Titirangi, West Auckland, since 1974. A keen observer of life's quirkier moments, he attended Owen Marshall's 1996 fiction writing course as a prelude to writing full-time.

**Judith Parker** was born in Echuca, Australia, in 1954 and raised and educated in Auckland. A former teacher and tractor driver, she now lives in Greytown and writes full-time. She has an MA (Hons) in Languages and Literature, has published a volume of poetry, Einstein's Widow (1995) and was shortlisted for the Reed Fiction Award in 1996.

**Gwenyth Perry** was born in Tauranga in 1942 and studied French and English at the University of Auckland. She has worked as a teacher, in radio and adult literacy. Her writing has been published in New Zealand and Singapore. Married with three adult children, she is currently working on literary research and is writing a novel.

**Vivienne Plumb** was born in Sydney in 1955 but has lived in Wellington for some years. Her collection of short stories, The Wife Who Spoke Japanese in Her Sleep, won the PEN Best First Book of Fiction Award in 1993 and her play, Love Knots, won the Bruce Mason Award in the same year. She is currently completing a BA.

**Sarah Quigley** was born in Christchurch in 1967. She has an MA from the University of Canterbury and a DPhil from Oxford. Her stories have been published in Takahe and Poetry New Zealand, and in 1996 she won the Listener short story writing contest. She is currently working on a biography of poet and editor Charles Brasch.

**Toni Quinlan** was born in 1918 and convent educated. She is a retired secretary/housewife, painter and fabric artist who has come lately to writing. She has had newspaper articles and poems published, has won painting awards and been placed in short story writing competitions. She enjoys black humour.

**Simon Robinson** was born in Melbourne in 1970 and grew up in Sydney. He left Australia in 1994 and now lives in Mt Eden, Auckland. He enjoys mountain climbing, reading, history, architecture and languages. Since 1995 he has been the New Zealand correspondent for *TIME* magazine.

**Jan Rooke** was born in London in 1955 and emigrated to New Zealand in 1996 with her husband, three sons, three cats and a dog. She is a psychiatric nurse whose interests include ancient history, myths and legends, cooking and cross-stitch.

**Joan Rosier-Jones** was born and educated in Christchurch. After a time in Wellington and London, she now writes and teaches on Auckland's North Shore. She is the author of a book on how to write your family history and four novels, the most recent of which is *Mother Tongue* (David Ling, 1996).

**John C. Ross** was born in Wellington in 1938. He has an MA from Victoria University and a PhD from the University of London. He worked for External Affairs then taught in London for four years before taking up his current position as lecturer in English at Massey University. His interests are reading, amateur theatre and tramping.

**Elspeth Sandys** was born and educated in Dunedin. After graduating MA from the University of Auckland she lived for twenty-one years in England. Prior to becoming a full-time writer she worked as an actress, teacher and editor. She has published six novels and a collection of short stories. Her latest novel is *Riding to Jerusalem* (Hodder Moa Beckett, 1996).

**Frank Sargeson** (1903–1982) was born in Hamilton. After leaving school he qualified as a solicitor, travelled to Europe then returned to New Zealand determined to become a full-time fiction writer. In his Takapuna bach he wrote novels, plays and short stories. His *Collected Stories* is considered a classic of New Zealand literature.

**Anita Seccombe** was born in 1943 and educated at Auckland Diocesan School. The mother of four adult children, she has managed a private business college and been actively involved with the Girl Guides Association. Her stories have been read on radio and published in the children's magazine *Allsorts*.

**Iain Sharp** was born in Glasgow, Scotland, in 1953. He emigrated to New Zealand as a boy and now lives in Auckland, working as a freelance journalist and reviewer. He has published three slim volumes of poetry and his short stories have appeared in *Landfall* and *Sport*.

**Tina Shaw** grew up in the Waikato and now lives in Devonport, Auckland. She has had short stories published in several New Zealand literary periodicals. Her first novel, *Birdie*, was published by David Ling in 1996 and received enthusiastic reviews.

**Dawn Sheppard** was born in Dannevirke in 1929. She has lived in Wellington, Dunedin, Marlborough and Feilding. A retired teacher of English and history, she has five children and eleven grandchildren, and has taught creative writing through the Feilding Community Learning Centre. Her interests are reading, writing and family.

**Noel Simpson** was born in Leeston in 1935 and educated in Christchurch. After spending some years truck driving and doing farm work, he attended Victoria University of Wellington and became a chartered accountant. Now living in semi-retirement at Paraparaumu Beach, he recently discovered the pleasures of writing and is a member of the Kapiti U3A writing class.

**Janette Sinclair** was born in Dunedin in 1948. She attended schools in Portobello, Fiji and Christchurch, and graduated MA in Sociology from the University of Canterbury. She now works as a survey designer in Wellington. Her stories have appeared in *Landfall*, *Metro*, *Sport* and *Quote Unquote*, and her novel, *In Touch*, was published in 1995.

**Elizabeth Smyth** was born in Christchurch in 1960. She has a degree in art theory and teaches this subject at tertiary level. She paints and writes fiction. In 1996 she studied creative writing under Sue McCauley, and in 1997 hopes to continue teaching and writing.

**David Somerset** was born in Oxford, Canterbury. He is an ex-teacher, ex-broadcaster and a 'scribbler'. He has written many radio scripts and other works, including photo stories and children's writing. His interests include hiking across remote regions of the globe.

**Garry Sommerville** was born in Mosgiel in 1952 and educated in Suva and at Victoria University of Wellington. He has lived in Asia, South America, Parnell, Freemans Bay, and Paremoremo and Manawatu prisons, and has a BA. He has also been a wharfie, truck driver, builder, fisherman, drug dealer, jail librarian and surfer. He now lives in the Far North.

**Britta Stabenow** was born in Germany in 1953. Raised and educated in Hamburg and Heidelberg, she settled in New Zealand in 1989. She lives in Timaru, works as a translator and began writing after taking the 1994 Aoraki fiction writing course. The 'Floe Riders' is her second published story.

**Gordon Stevens** was born in Methven in 1955 and raised on a Canterbury farm. After schooling at Timaru Boys' High he worked as a meat inspector, circus hand, bus driver and shepherd. In 1995 he took a media course at Nelson Polytech and became interested in creative writing. He lives in Christchurch.

**Mary Stuart** was born in Dunedin in 1914 but has spent most of her life in Wellington. She was educated at Columba College and Marsden School. Her interests include theatre, travel, swimming and golf, as well as her many grandchildren and great-grandchildren, for whom she writes her stories.

**Dianne Taylor** was born in 1962 and lives in Ponsonby, Auckland. She worked for fifteen years as an advertising copywriter and is now a student at the University of Auckland, majoring in English and Film Studies. She is the mother of two young daughters. Her interests are short story writing and writing for film.

**Rosemary Tearle** was born in Whakatane in 1944 and educated in Auckland, Fiji and Wellington. Her interests are writing, reading, campervanning, tramping, kite-fishing and gardening. She lives in Mt Eden, Auckland.

**Jon Thomas** was born in London in 1937 and came to New Zealand in 1973. In 1987 he abandoned engineering for the 'Ninety Mile Beach lifestyle', and now fishes and writes. His work has been published in *Poetry New Zealand*, *Takahe* and *Antipodean Tales*. He won the *Sunday Star* short story contest in 1993.

**Virginia Were** lives in Devonport, Auckland. She was a member of the cult band Marie and the Atom. Her work has been published in literary journals in New Zealand and Australia, and she won the PEN Best First Book of Poetry Award for her collection *Juliet Bravo Juliet*.

**Jane Westaway** was born in London in 1948. She lives in Wellington and is a writer, reviewer and journalist. She was awarded a *Reader's Digest*-PEN-Stout Fellowship in 1993 and a Children's Writing Bursary in 1994. Her short stories have been antholgised and broadcast, and a collection for young adults, *Reliable Friendly Girls* (Longacre Press), was published in 1996.

**Judith White** was conceived in a caravan in Methven, born in Wellington and educated in Hastings. After working as a laboratory technician she travelled nomadically for five years. Married with two children and living in Auckland, she is the author of a short story collection, *Visiting Ghosts* (1991), and in 1996 shared the Sargeson Writer's Fellowship.

**Steve Whitehouse** was born in 1945, raised in Wellington and attended Hutt Valley High and Victoria University. He lives in New York, produces TV documentaries for the United Nations and dabbles in fiction writing and journalism. He is thought to be the only winner of the Hutt Valley Hutt School Molly Campbell Shield for Literature to have opened the batting for Cyprus (101) vs Bahrain in 1984.

**Ian Williams** was born in London and emigrated to New Zealand in 1959. He worked for New Zealand Railways and the National Airways Corporation before becoming an advertising copywriter. Now in his late fifties, he lives in Palmerston North. 'Stuart' is his first published story.

**Louise Wrightson** was born in 1949 and lives in Wilton, Wellington. Her story, 'Salvation', won the *Quote Unquote* short short story contest in 1996. Her short stories are getting longer and her poetry is getting leaner. Her company, New Zealand Books Abroad, sells New Zealand books all over the world.

**Ben Yong** was born in Wellington in 1974. He has a BA in English literature and Mandarin and is currently studying law at Victoria University. His interests include reading and translating Chinese literature.